LAD

For there is no friend
like a sister in calm or
stormy weather

–Christina Rossetti

MYSTERIES *of* LANCASTER COUNTY

Another's Treasure

ANOTHER'S TREASURE

MYSTERIES *of* LANCASTER COUNTY

Nancy Mehl

Guideposts

New York

Mysteries of Lancaster County is a trademark of Guideposts.

Published by Guideposts Books & Inspirational Media
110 William Street
New York, NY 10038
Guideposts.org

Cover and interior design by Müllerhaus
Cover illustration by Bob Kayganich, represented by Deborah Wolfe, LTD.
Typeset by Aptara, Inc.

Printed and bound in the United States of America
10 9 8 7 6 5 4 3 2

ANOTHER'S TREASURE

CHAPTER ONE

Elizabeth Classen stood on the front porch of the old Victorian house that had been in her family for generations. She ran her fingers lightly over the porch railing. She remembered standing out here with her father when she was a child, watching shooting stars streak across the sky.

She breathed deeply of the early morning April air, which bore the scent of rich, tilled earth and newly leafing trees. As the sun peeked over the edges of Pennsylvania's rolling hills and Amish farmlands, it cast a pinkish glow on the idyllic countryside. Elizabeth loved Pennsylvania, and she loved her family home, situated on the outskirts of the village of Bird-in-Hand, deep in the heart of Lancaster County's Amish country. Moving back ten years ago, taking care of her mother and running their shop after her father died, had been an easy choice. Now, though, living here without her mother felt odd. Elizabeth kept expecting to see Mama sitting in her favorite chair, reading a book or knitting something for someone in the family.

Reddy, the Classens' rooster, suddenly crowed to welcome the dawn. Elizabeth smiled. She loved to hear his morning greeting.

The screen door squeaked and a voice said, "You're up early."

Elizabeth turned to find her sister Mary standing behind her. Mary held out a cup of coffee. "Thought you could use this."

"Thanks." Elizabeth gratefully accepted the steaming cup.

Mary came up next to her. "It seems so strange to be standing here again. Mama and Daddy both gone now." As they looked out over the horizon, Rachel Fischer, an Amish farmer's wife and their closest neighbor to the east, passed by in her horse-drawn buggy. Her eight-year-old twin boys, Thomas and Matthew, flanked her on either side. They all exchanged a wave.

Elizabeth sighed as Rachel's buggy disappeared around a bend in the road. "I know. I was just thinking the same thing. I feel a little guilty, you know," she said softly. "Asking you and Martha to give up so much."

Mary gave her sister a gentle squeeze. "Oh, Lizzie. You didn't disrupt our lives. We both needed a change. I hated working for that grocery store. On my feet all day. I enjoyed talking to customers, but we never had time for a real conversation. Everything moved so quickly. Taking over the family business is... Well, it's just perfect. And now, maybe I can paint again. Who knows? Perhaps someday we can even sell my work in our store."

Elizabeth chuckled. "Your goal is to sell your beautiful pictures in a thrift store?"

Mary laughed. "Hey, selling a painting anywhere would be great. Now, let's get going. We need to be ready when our customers flood in."

"I'd like to believe for a flood, but at this point, even a trickle would be welcome. I'm not sure why we fought so hard to keep this place and reopen the store."

"Yes, you are. Because it's…ours. Because Daddy and Mama loved it. Our great-grandmother started it so long ago. How could we sell our land, our family's homestead, and the store to…strangers? This is our heritage." She patted Elizabeth's shoulder. "Martha and I came back because we love this place too, sis. We want this just as much as you do."

Mary turned to go inside, but Elizabeth caught her by the arm. "But what about your kids? Won't you and Martha miss them and your grandkids?"

Her sisters had given up much more than she had to come home. They both had children, although neither was married anymore. Mary's husband had left her five years ago for a younger woman, and Martha's beloved husband, Chuck, died two years ago from a heart attack. They'd both left family behind in Kansas and Indiana to come to Bird-in-Hand and take over the family business. She was so thankful for them. Now there were voices in the house again. Noise. It had been too quiet since Mama had gone. It had only been a few months since cancer had taken her, but it seemed like an eternity.

Mary grabbed her hand. "Of course we will, but we can't live our lives through them. It isn't healthy for us or for them. Frankly, I was starting to get a little clingy. Cheese-n-crackers, Lizzy, I don't want to be one of *those* mothers."

Elizabeth smiled at her sister's use of "cheese-n-crackers," a phrase their mother had taught them. *"Classens don't swear,"* she'd said once when Mary repeated a bad word she'd heard at school. *"If you must say something when you're upset, why don't you just say…cheese-n-crackers?"*

Elizabeth wiped away a tear evoked by the memory. "Maybe if I'd married or had children I wouldn't have felt so purposeless before I moved back home after Daddy died. But taking care of Mama made me feel useful. Needed." And because of staffing changes ten years ago, the timing had seemed exactly right to leave her administrative assistant job at a hospital in Harrisburg to care for her mother and help her in the store.

"And you took care of her so well, even keeping the store open for five years together with her. Now we're going to make the store thrive again, in Mama's honor," Mary said.

"Yes." Elizabeth nodded in agreement. "It broke her heart to close, and she urged me to reopen one day. Now here we are..."

Elizabeth took one more deep breath of the country air and followed Mary into the house. Martha was in the kitchen, standing over the stove, cooking a skillet full of eggs.

"Oh, Martha," Mary said. "I told you I bought muffins for breakfast. You didn't need to do this."

"Nonsense," Martha said huffily. "We need a nice hot breakfast to give us energy for today. Besides, I haven't gone to a lot of trouble. It's just bacon and eggs. Toast. Oh, and hash browns."

Elizabeth laughed, then said, "We aren't getting ready to drive a team of horses through the fields for spring planting like Farmer Lapp, Sister."

As Martha pushed back a strand of brown hair from her forehead, Elizabeth marveled at how her beauty had only increased with age. She was fifty-five, with bright blue eyes set in a delicate face. Martha had a lively disposition, always busy accomplishing some kind of task, whether big or small. Like their biblical namesakes, Martha was a doer, whereas Mary, the youngest of the three sisters, was a dreamer. Sensitive, adventurous, and sometimes careless, Mary was more likely to leap before she looked, unlike Martha and Elizabeth. Frankly, Elizabeth couldn't understand why any man would leave someone like Mary. Elizabeth had always envied her. She'd never been free and easy. As the oldest sister, Elizabeth had always felt responsible. For everyone.

Knowing better than to argue with Martha, the two sisters sat down at the rustic wooden table made by their father and ate a quick breakfast. Of course, it was delicious. Martha was an incredible cook.

After getting dressed, the sisters tended to the animals. Mary had brought her dachshund, Tinkerbelle, with her, and Martha had added her cat, Butterscotch. Their mother's border collie, Pal, added one more dog to the mix. Besides the domestic animals, their mother had also accumulated three pygmy goats. Then there were the hens...and Reddy the rooster. As long as Elizabeth could remember, the Classens had owned chickens. Fresh eggs were a staple in their household.

"Only four eggs this morning," Mary called out as she came in the front door. She carried a basket into the kitchen and put it on the counter. "I fed all the outdoor animals."

"Thank you, Mary," Martha said, "but you don't have to do that every morning. We can help."

Mary shrugged. "We all help in our own ways. I don't mind feeding the outside animals and getting the eggs. In fact, I enjoy it. Besides, Elizabeth feeds the inside animals. It all works out."

"Well, I still appreciate it."

"Time's a wastin'," Elizabeth called out. "Let's get out to the barn."

Elizabeth tried to ignore the nervous butterflies in her stomach as the sisters walked toward the big barn that had been converted to a combined thrift store and gift shop. She looked at her sisters. Mary wore jeans, boots, and a nice white blouse. Her blond hair was tucked behind her ears and fell softly on her shoulders. Martha wore slacks and a light purple sweater, perfect for the nippy spring weather. Elizabeth glanced down at her plain brown skirt, blue blouse, and no-nonsense loafers. Mary liked to tease her that she took after their grandparents who were once Conservative Mennonites. Her sisters urged her to try more modern clothes, but for now, she was comfortable as she was.

When they reached the barn, Elizabeth unlocked it and pulled the door back. The sign over the entrance read SECONDHAND BLESSINGS. Inside were rows of tables and shelves. On one side of the store were all the clothing racks. At the back were appliances and dishes. Other sections included household goods, crafts, decorative items, tools, and jewelry. Many of the tables in the middle of the store contained miscellaneous items that didn't fit a larger category. A section at the front of the store had shelves filled with handcrafts and gift items, most made by their Amish neighbors and friends.

On a table near the checkout counter, Martha had added some baked items. Banana nut bread, zucchini bread, lemon poppy seed bread, and cranberry bread loaves were encased in plastic wrap and labeled. It was a new venture for the re-opening of the store. After jumping through some hoops with the health department, the sisters had won approval to sell food. Mary had suggested that, down the road, they offer lunch items, and maybe set up a couple of tables and some chairs for dining, but Elizabeth wasn't sure it was a good idea. They'd shelved that plan for now.

Elizabeth grabbed three aprons and handed one to each sister. Then she slipped into hers.

Mary went over to a table in the middle of the room. "The things we got from the Smucker estate sale should go quickly. Especially the candleholders and the china. Even the bric-a-brac is classy."

"A lot of the pieces had to be cleaned and polished," Elizabeth said. "Ruth helped me with that. It was so kind of her." Ruth Zook was the wife of the pastor of Mount Zion Mennonite Church.

"How's Pastor Zook feeling?" Martha asked. "He looked so frail last Sunday."

Elizabeth shrugged. "Just getting older as far as I know." She sighed. "Ruth told me recently that she wished he could retire, but they just couldn't afford it."

Mary, who'd been straightening one of the shelves, snapped her fingers. "I can't believe I forgot to tell you this," she said. "You know Darlene, the waitress over at the Two Bird Café?"

"Sure."

"She told me that she heard a rumor that Ruth and Pastor Zook are retiring from the church. Going to Florida."

Elizabeth frowned. "That doesn't make sense. Ruth told me they didn't have the money to leave Bird-in-Hand just a couple of weeks ago or so. What could happen in such a short time that would change everything? And why wouldn't Ruth tell me that herself? It's probably just a rumor."

"Maybe their children are helping them," Martha said. "It's not really our business anyway."

"I realize it's not our business," Elizabeth said. "I'm just curious."

"Well, I think we should be glad for them," Mary said. "They've both worked very hard for many years. He was Mama and Daddy's pastor too."

"I *am* glad for them." Elizabeth was beginning to feel a little frustrated. Sometimes her sisters had a way of turning things she said into opinions she didn't actually have.

"Well, that's just great," Mary said suddenly.

"What's wrong?" Elizabeth asked.

Mary, who'd bent over, stood up. "I found this old photograph on the floor, under the table with the Smucker items. I think it went with the frame we sold to Dorothy Mulligan. I can't believe she tossed it on the floor like this."

"That's Dorothy for you. She acts the same way at church dinners. Leaves her dirty dishes behind for others to pick up."

"She also takes the last of something without checking to see if anyone else wants it," Martha grumbled.

Elizabeth sighed. "You're never going to forgive her for eating the last of Essie Baldwin's cobbler, are you?"

"Oh my goodness, Martha," Mary said. "Are you still mad about that? You were a teenager then!"

Martha drew herself up as straight as a board. "She knew I hadn't had any, but she rushed over to the table, practically knocking me down, so she could get that last piece. It was incredibly rude."

"Your cobbler is one hundred times better than hers," Elizabeth said with a sigh. "You didn't miss anything."

"Maybe not, but it was the attitude behind it that irritated me."

Elizabeth shook her head. "Okay, now back to the picture. What did the frame look like? I can't quite remember."

"Silver with lots of rhinestones," Mary said. "Really fancy."

"Really tacky," Elizabeth added. "But she liked it. I guess that's all that matters. Give me the picture. I'll check with Anita Smucker to see if it's something she wants."

Mary handed Elizabeth the picture. "I doubt she wants it, or she wouldn't have left it in the frame. Besides, it's not a great photo."

Elizabeth glanced at the picture. It looked really old. As Mary said, not a great shot, but Dorothy shouldn't have thrown it on the floor. What was wrong with some people? Sighing, she slid it into her apron pocket. Then she turned toward the entrance as she heard someone drive up quickly and stop, their brakes squealing. Seconds later, a woman rushed into the barn, her face ashen and her eyes wild. Elizabeth immediately recognized her. It was Anita, the Smuckers' daughter. She'd organized the estate sale after her father died. "Can we help you, Anita?"

Anita pointed a finger at her. "I need it back," she said shakily. "Now."

Elizabeth walked toward her. "Need what back?" she asked. "I'm afraid I don't understand."

"I need it back," she repeated. "Everything. All the things I brought from my parents' house. I have to have it all back!"

CHAPTER TWO

Elizabeth hurried up next to the agitated woman. "I—I don't understand," she said.

Anita shook her thin finger at the sisters. "Please! I beg you! Gather it up. Now." She looked around at the tables and shelves full of items. "Where are my things?"

"Some of them are here," Martha said, pointing at the table with the remainder of the Smuckers' donations. "But we already sold—"

"Already?" Anita shrieked wildly. "How could you sell them so soon?"

Elizabeth had had enough of the drama. "You gave them to us to sell."

Anita took several deep breaths and seemed unable to respond. Elizabeth turned toward her sisters and said, "Continue to prepare for the opening. I'm taking Anita into the house to see if we can sort this out. And for goodness' sake, remove everything we still have of hers. Don't sell anything else."

"I need it all immediately," Anita demanded.

"We'll gather what we still have. Bring everything inside once you gather it together, Martha," Elizabeth instructed.

She began to lead Anita toward the house. Of all the times for her to go on a silly rampage. Why now? Why the morning of their official opening? Maybe she could calm Anita down and find out just what was really going on.

When they got inside, Elizabeth guided Anita over to the kitchen table and helped her into a chair. She broke out one of the banana nut muffins Mary had purchased for breakfast, put it on a small plate, and poured a cup of coffee. Thankfully, it was still hot. Once she'd put the coffee cup on the table in front of Anita, she sat down next to her.

"Now tell me what happened between the time you brought us your family's belongings and this morning."

Anita took a sip of coffee before sighing deeply as if trying to calm herself. "It was the letter. A letter in the old family Bible."

Elizabeth nodded. "Okay. So you found a letter that upset you? Can you tell me what it said?"

"I'll do better than that," Anita snapped. She reached into her jacket pocket and pulled out a folded piece of paper, then handed it to Elizabeth, who carefully opened it.

My dear daughter, it read, *although I have left all my worldly possessions to you, one of them is worth more than everything else I own combined. It's truly a treasure. I know you love my riddles, so I want to leave you with one more. Here it is:*

When lightning speaks and feathers fly,
And your mother's sister's child makes dirty pies,
You'll find yourself feeling quite continental.
Open your eyes and you'll see the truth.
Hidden in shadows and very sentimental.

When you find the treasure, you'll see why it is so valuable. Although it has been in our family for many years, it is time for it to find a new home. I'm certain you won't have any trouble finding a buyer. You should be well taken care of the rest of your life. Just remember how much I love you, dearest Anita.

It was signed, *Your loving father.*

"Why would he leave you a riddle?" Elizabeth asked. "Why not just tell you what the treasure is?"

"He was suffering from some dementia toward the end. But he also loved riddles, and when I was a kid, he was always making me solve them. He thought figuring them out made me smarter. Frankly, they only made me crazy, but I couldn't tell him. It would have hurt him." She shrugged her slight shoulders. "They seemed harmless. But this..." She pointed at the letter. "This is just...cruel."

"If he was sick, I'm sure he didn't realize how challenging this might be," Elizabeth said gently. "He probably thought it would be fun. Something to cheer you up after his death."

Anita groaned. "Well, it's not working. I miss my father. And I just might be missing out on an important inheritance."

"But why do you think *we* have this...object?"

She shook her head. "I'm not sure you do, but some of the things I gave you on consignment were possessions Daddy always said should never be sold. I suspect the reason is that one of them is the item he's referring to in his letter."

Elizabeth bit her lip to keep from expressing her frustration. "So why did you part with them?"

"Because there's hardly any money in the bank. I mean, the house is worth quite a bit, but I don't want to let it go if I don't absolutely have to. It's been in our family for three gener-ations. I thought selling some of the more expensive stuff, things I have no real attachment to, might help."

"But shouldn't they have gone to an auction house if they were worth that much? Why give them to us? A secondhand store?"

Anita sighed and brushed her graying bangs from her slen-der face. "I have some possessions going to auction. Furniture. Larger items. Some things I know are valuable, such as the family silver. What I gave you were items that weren't worth as much but that I hoped would give me some money to live on until after the auctions. I might have the Smucker name, but our wing of the family is only a distant relation to the famous jelly-making ones. We can't lay claim to any of their money."

Elizabeth nodded. "I understand. But how can you be ab-solutely certain you gave us the object your father alluded to? Couldn't it still be in your house?"

"I hired an appraiser to go through everything. There's nothing left of real value—nothing worth anything near what my father hinted at in his letter. You have to have it."

"We've already sold quite a few of your items, Anita. I don't remember your total so far, but it's a little over three hundred dollars."

Anita's eyes widened. "How could you have already sold things? I thought today was your grand opening."

"It is. They sold the other night. The night of the pre-sale party. The one we invited you to?"

"I knew there was a party," she said, "but you didn't tell me you were open for business."

Elizabeth gave her a tight smile. "We sent you a flyer that mentioned the folks from church and other invited guests would get first crack at our inventory. We did very well Friday night."

Anita's attempts to stay calm vanished like smoke in the wind, and she stood quickly. "You better get back every single item of mine you sold. If you don't retrieve them, I'll sue you for everything you've got. And I can do it. I'll contact my cousin Alf. He's an attorney."

She shot Elizabeth one last dirty look and stormed out of the house, almost tripping over Tinkerbelle, who yelped and looked offended. Elizabeth called the dachshund over and picked her up, trying to soothe her injured feelings before putting her down again. Then she sat in her chair for a while, thinking. She could hear Anita's car start and her tires spin on the road that led away from the barn. After a few minutes, she got up and headed back to the shop.

Mary and Martha waited outside the entrance to the barn, Pal sitting beside them.

"What's going on?" Martha asked. "Is everything okay?"

Elizabeth sighed and shook her head. "No, everything's not okay. We have to locate all the items we sold from the Smucker estate."

"We put what was left in a box," Mary said, "but Anita took off before we could give it to her."

"Give it to me, and I'll put it in the house," Elizabeth said. "We can't take a chance it will get mixed up with our inventory again."

Mary hurried inside the barn and came back with a large box, which she gave to Elizabeth. "The china's in another box, but it's heavy. I'll put it in the back where no one will see it. We can carry it in later."

"Okay," Elizabeth said. "I'll be right back."

As Elizabeth walked to the house, she noticed several cars turning off the main road and driving toward the barn. People were coming to their opening, which should have excited her, but Anita Smucker's suspicions and emotional rant had cast a pall over what should have been an exhilarating morning.

Instead of simply focusing on the opening of Secondhand Blessings, they would have to spend time chasing down every single item they'd sold that had belonged to the Smucker estate.

After placing the box inside the house, Elizabeth stepped back outside. She pasted a smile on her face as she walked to the barn. Why had this happened today of all days? Was their goal of keeping their family's dream alive doomed to fail before it even started?

CHAPTER THREE

The morning passed by quickly as shoppers and well-wishers came in and out of Secondhand Blessings. Mary enjoyed talking to everyone who visited the first day. They seemed excited to see the shop operating again, and several of their older visitors recounted stories from past visits when the sisters' grandmother Lois or their mother, Elma, ran the store.

Besides past customers, there were many new shoppers. Several people from the church stopped by too, even though they'd already seen the store.

"So how's it going?"

Mary jumped at the sound of a man's voice coming from behind her. Billy Richmond stood there, smiling at her. She hadn't seen him approach.

"Oh, Billy," she said. She cleared her throat, feeling nervous. His brown eyes sought hers. "We're doing well," she said, noticing a slight tremble in her words. She tried to gather her wits and steady her voice. "We sold quite a bit of merchandise this morning. The afternoon has been busy too."

"I'm glad." He held up a toaster that looked brand new. "My old toaster has one setting left. Charcoal. I think it's time to make a change."

Mary grinned at his joke. "I think this one will give you a couple more options."

He stared at her for a moment as they both fell silent. Billy, a man her family had known for years, was a local contractor and had helped fix up the old barn so they could reopen the store. Mary and Billy had been friends when they were young, but now that they were adults, their relationship had changed. Although they'd spoken a couple of times since Mary moved home, she felt rather shy around him. Now in his fifties, he reminded Mary of a younger Harrison Ford—handsome, witty, and kind. She felt drawn to him . . . and afraid of him all at the same time. Billy had dark hair and deep brown eyes with eyelashes most women would covet. He was muscular and not very tall. Nothing like Brian, who was tall, blond, and on the thin side. Yet when she looked at Billy, Brian's face floated in front of her. Would she always think of Brian when she was around other men?

Mary nodded toward Elizabeth, who stood at the front of the barn next to the cash register. "Elizabeth can check you out."

Billy said goodbye and headed toward the front. Mary watched him as he paid for the toaster and left. It was likely for the best that they hadn't talked much, she told herself. She sure wasn't ready to let another man in her life. Maybe she never would be.

The sisters closed the store at five o'clock. Elizabeth and Mary straightened up the merchandise while Martha looked over the receipts and counted the money. When they were done, they went inside the house and gathered around their large kitchen table. The homey kitchen expressed their parents' personalities. The old stove had belonged to their grandmother. It was huge. White enamel with black edging, it was a definite antique. But no new stove could bake as well. The kitchen cabinets had been crafted by their father. Solid wood, though Elizabeth had painted them white. Their mother had mounted several large copper cake forms on the wall, and they added to the overall ambience of the large, comfortable room.

"So how did we do?" Elizabeth asked.

Martha and Mary sat down while Elizabeth got a pitcher of lemonade out of the refrigerator and poured it into three glasses.

Martha looked at them over the top of her spectacles. She only wore them when she read or when she worked on the books. Martha was the sister with math and money skills. She peered down at her notebook and smiled. "I'm happy to say we did very well. After paying our sellers, we netted a little over four hundred dollars."

Mary frowned. "That doesn't sound like much."

Elizabeth shook her head. "For our first day, it's very good. People are still feeling us out. I think once we get in more big-ticket items, our profits will increase."

"Amos Benson is very interested in that old armoire we have in the back," Mary said. "I think he might buy it. We could make a tidy sum on that."

Elizabeth smiled. "See? I'm confident sales will pick up." She looked at Martha. "We sold almost all of your bread. Maybe we could expand our baked goods?"

Martha grunted. "If someone helps me. I can't spend all my time baking."

"I'll help," Mary said.

Martha sighed. "You usually lose interest when you get bored. I'll need you to see it through."

Mary's mouth dropped open. "Since when do I not see things through? When we were teenagers? I've grown up a bit since then, you know."

The corners of Martha's mouth twitched. "Okay, you're right. I'm sorry. Why don't we come up with a menu of items? We can do some baking tonight and make a plan for the rest of the week."

"All right."

Elizabeth couldn't hold back a smile. Mary's irritation with her sister was already gone. She never stayed mad long.

Martha got up and took some cookies from the cookie jar, put them on a plate, and set it on the table. "Sorry, but talking about baking made me hungry." She sat down and took a cookie. "I saw you talking to Billy Richmond today, Mary. What did he want?"

Mary looked down at the table. Elizabeth was aware that her sister still carried deep wounds caused by Brian's desertion. His secretary was much younger than Mary, although certainly not as attractive. Elizabeth was certain she was after Brian's money. She remembered how devastated Mary had been when he left. The pain he'd caused his wife and his children was something she would never forget. Thankfully, Michael and Jennifer were doing well. Michael had recently married and had a child on the way. He refused to see his father. Jennifer was in college and, as far as Elizabeth knew, also had no contact with Brian.

Realizing it was time to change the subject, Elizabeth got up and grabbed a notepad from a kitchen drawer, found a pen, and sat down at the table. "Even though I hate to bring it up, we've got to deal with the Anita Smucker situation."

Martha sighed in exasperation. "That woman! She actually threatened to sue us?"

Elizabeth nodded. "Her cousin really is an attorney. I've met him. He's…" She shut her mouth tight, trying to find something to say about him that wasn't judgmental.

"Mama always told us that if we couldn't say something nice, not to say anything at all," Mary said. "This guy must be awful."

"Let's just say that Alf Marston isn't a very nice person."

"How do you know him, Lizzie?" Martha asked.

"He came to a church dinner once. Anita introduced us." She paused for a moment and looked away, trying to find the right words. "Let's just say I wasn't impressed and let it go at that."

"But how could they sue us?" Mary asked. "We haven't done anything wrong."

"I honestly don't know," Elizabeth replied. "But if we don't want to find out, we need to get back everything we sold that belonged to the Smuckers. Once we turn it all over to her, she should be satisfied and leave us alone."

"But we'll have to buy the items back," Martha said. "There goes our profit."

Elizabeth shrugged. "I understand what you're saying, but it's better we lose a little profit than lose our store."

Mary took a quick breath and blew it out forcefully. "I still can't believe Warren Smucker actually left his daughter a ridiculous riddle to solve instead of just telling her about this so-called treasure."

Elizabeth arched one eyebrow. "Warren really loved jokes and riddles. He told Mama once that he believed his riddles helped Anita do better in school. That they made her think better. I suspect once he began to experience dementia, leaving his daughter one last riddle made sense to him."

"Well, if she's so smart, why doesn't she just figure out the riddle and leave the rest of us alone?" Martha snapped.

"Mama also said Anita was never very good with riddles," Elizabeth said, chuckling. "It seems she really hated them, but Warren fooled himself into thinking she liked them as much as he did." She took a sip of lemonade and picked up her cookie. "One thing we need to keep in mind is that this riddle might not make any sense. I hope it helps us, but if not, we'll just have to locate all of Anita's belongings and turn them over to her. After that, it's up to her to figure it out." She pointed at Martha. "Let's make a list of everything that's been sold and who bought it." She sighed deeply. "Then we'll contact each and every person and ask them to let us buy the piece back. It will be a little awkward, but at this point, what other choice do we have?"

Martha and Mary didn't argue with their older sister, but Elizabeth knew they weren't happy about this turn of events. Neither was she. Could one of their customers be aware that they were holding on to an extremely valuable object? If so, what would happen if they refused to return it?

CHAPTER FOUR

Martha went through the inventory list item by item. "So one of these things is supposed to be worth a lot of money?" The doubt was clear in her voice.

Elizabeth nodded. "That's what Anita said, but honestly, I just don't see it." She got up and brought the box of Anita's belongings over to the table. Then she pointed at the box of china still on the floor that Mary and Martha had carried in. "Now the china is nice, but I looked it up online. It's worth a few hundred dollars. That's it." She reached into the other box and pulled out the first thing she found. "Two candlesticks," she said. "*Silver-plated.* Not pure silver." She set those aside and reached into the box again. "These two statues, a male shepherd and a female…"

"Shepherdess," Martha intoned, staring at Elizabeth over her glasses.

"Yes, thank you. I know." Elizabeth shook her head. "These are nice, but I doubt they're worth a lot."

Mary got up and grabbed her laptop from a small built-in desk in the corner of the kitchen. She flipped it open and pointed at the statues. "Read the name of the maker on the bottom?"

"They're signed by Axel Locher, a Bing and Grondahl artist," Martha said. "I already researched them. They're worth around four hundred dollars. With Anita's permission, we priced them at five hundred."

"People will really pay that much for secondhand items like this?" Mary asked, frowning. "Seems like a lot."

"Antique dealers scour secondhand stores," Elizabeth said. "Of course, they're hoping the store owners don't realize the value of the antiques they sell." She shook her head as she gazed at her sister. "I already explained this to you, didn't I?"

"Yeah, you did. I still find it hard to believe."

"Well, believe it," Martha interjected. "I saw a couple in the store this morning that I'm sure were dealers."

"How could you tell?" Mary asked.

"They picked up all the collectibles and checked the bottom for markings. I expect they'll be back soon."

Mary rolled her eyes. "Okay, point taken. What's next?"

Elizabeth pulled out several more items, including a pitcher, some salt and pepper shakers, two lace tablecloths, some silver serving spoons, and three framed pictures of angels—nothing that looked very valuable. The frames around the angels reminded her of something. "What about that frame that Dorothy Mulligan bought? You know, the one with the picture she tossed on the floor? How much do you think it's worth?"

Martha shook her head. "It was silver-plated and extremely gaudy. Covered in cheap rhinestones. Certainly not valuable."

Elizabeth sighed and wrote down Dorothy Mulligan's name on her pad. "Okay, what's next?"

"Wait a minute," Mary said. "How do you know they were rhinestones? Could they have been jewels?"

Martha laughed. "Trust me, that horrible thing has no value. I'd stake my life on it."

Mary didn't look convinced, but she shrugged and nodded at Martha to continue.

Martha started reading through the list again, mentioning several items purchased at the church sale, none of them worth much. "Oh, here's Ruth Zook." Martha peered carefully at the notation on the page and then riffled through the pages. "Yes, here it is. Ruth bought that bracelet. You know the one with all the white and green rhinestones?"

"Maybe that's it," Mary said. "What if those weren't rhinestones?"

Martha grunted. "You think every rhinestone is a valuable jewel." Her forehead furrowed with concern. "I'm certain it was just costume jewelry. I guess I'd sooner believe the bracelet was real than that old frame. But if the stones were real, they'd be worth..." She stopped and looked over at Elizabeth. "My goodness. One of the green stones was huge. If it was an emerald..."

"But it couldn't be." Elizabeth thought for a moment. "Where did we get the value for that piece?"

"From Anita," Martha said. "She told me it was collectible costume jewelry. Since there wasn't any kind of a mark on it, I took her word for it. She's the one who set the value."

Mary snapped her fingers. "That's got to be it! That's the piece Mr. Smucker was talking about."

"But what about the riddle?" Elizabeth asked. "It doesn't fit."

"Do you remember it?" Mary asked.

"Yes. I wrote it down right after Anita read it to me. Hold on a minute." Elizabeth went over to a drawer in the kitchen and opened it. She grabbed a folded piece of paper, closed the drawer, and opened the sheet. After reading it out loud, she put it on the kitchen table.

"Well, I don't get it," Mary replied huffily. "But it's got to fit somehow. This has to be it."

"I hate to say it," Martha said, "but Mary may be right." She blinked several times and cleared her throat. "You know, suddenly the Zooks have the money to go to Florida. I mean, could it be…"

"Oh, Martha!" Elizabeth exclaimed. "Ruth Zook would have told us if she found out the piece had real gems. She's a very honest woman."

"Sometimes people lie," Mary said softly. "People you would never suspect of being dishonest."

Elizabeth knew Mary wasn't just talking about Ruth now. "I know that, sweetie," she said gently. "But I don't believe Ruth would do something like this. I really don't."

Martha decisively shut the ledger, causing a loud thumping sound. "Well, there's only one way to find out. We ask for the bracelet back. If she still has it and she gives it to us, we'll know she didn't sell it so she and Pastor Zook could retire to Florida. But if she doesn't have it…"

"I still have a hard time believing she's guilty, but I suppose anything is possible." Elizabeth was trying to be supportive of Ruth, a woman she'd come to admire over the years. However, Martha had made some good points. Could the bracelet really be what Anita was looking for?

"Should we finish the list?" Mary asked. "I mean, if the bracelet turns out to be costume jewelry, we haven't accomplished much, have we?"

"No, I suppose you're right," Elizabeth said. She read through the rest of the articles sold from the Smucker estate. Most of them were small items. "Here's something. Uriah Barnhart bought that old Civil War sword. What if it was worth more than we realized?"

"I thought Uriah Barnhart moved away," Mary said.

"He left for about a year," Elizabeth replied, "but he came back a few months ago. I was surprised when he showed up at the church sale."

"I did a search on that sword," Martha said. "But to be honest, I couldn't find anything exactly like it. Again, I took Anita's word for it that it wasn't worth very much."

"We sold it for one hundred dollars." Elizabeth stared at her sister. "What would it be worth if it was a significant antique?"

Martha shook her head. "A little research on the internet doesn't make me an expert, but I didn't find anything that blew me away. Most of the swords I saw were valued in the hundreds of dollars. I did see one that was almost thirty thousand dollars, but that's certainly not more than what the Smuckers' estate is worth."

"Unless it was owned by someone famous," Mary said. "Maybe it was George Washington's sword."

"Oh, for goodness sake, Mary," Martha said. "George Washington didn't fight in the Civil War!"

"Well, forgive me for trying to help," Mary said, blushing. "I just wasn't thinking."

Martha shook her head. "I'm sorry, Sis. I'm just uptight about this stupid situation. I didn't mean to take it out on you."

Mary reached over and grabbed her sister's hand. "I know. It's all right." She looked over at Elizabeth. "Still, I think the sword's a possibility."

"You might be right," Elizabeth said with a grimace. "But who wants to contact Uriah? I know I don't."

Uriah Barnhart was a hermit who lived in one of the worst houses in Bird-in-Hand. It wasn't because he was poor. Uriah had been the president of a local grain company before he retired. It was widely known that he'd made a great deal of money with the company and that his pension was quite healthy. He hadn't had much to do with the residents of Bird-in-Hand before he retired, and since then his cantankerous personality had only served to further distance him from everyone. Uriah was a skinflint, tighter than a cheap girdle, and meaner than a wet hen. When he left town, most people were relieved, but his house was never sold, causing some to wonder if they were really rid of him. That question had been answered when he suddenly showed up again.

A soft mew caused Mary to look down. Martha's cat, Butterscotch, rubbed up against her leg. She leaned down and scratched his head. His loud purring made the sisters smile.

"Maybe Uriah's just lonely," Mary said.

"I've lived here longer than you," Elizabeth said. "I'm telling you that after he retired, he became just plain mean. The only person I ever saw him treat like a human being was Mama. I have no idea why, but he was always kind to her."

"Was Mama nice to him?" Mary asked.

Elizabeth nodded. "Always. Not that we saw him much, but when we did, he was a different person. To her anyway. Not to me. He always had something nasty to say to me."

"Wonder why he came back?"

"I have no idea. Like I said, I was shocked to see him Friday night. He rarely goes out. He hasn't been to church in years."

"How did he find out about our event?" Mary asked.

Elizabeth shrugged. "I have no idea."

"Perhaps he wanted some company," Martha said.

Elizabeth shook her head. "Not likely. He looked around for a few minutes, grabbed the sword, paid for it, and left. Never said boo to any of us. And I've never heard of him paying a hundred dollars for *anything* before."

"Maybe he realized the sword was worth a lot more than we were asking and figured he could get a deal."

"I hope not," Elizabeth said. "That would mean he probably won't let us buy it back."

The sisters were silent as they considered the repercussions.

"Wait a minute," Mary said finally. "Remember that we marked it at one hundred dollars because Anita told us to. If we sold it for less than it's really worth, it isn't our fault. It's hers. Just like the bracelet."

"But how do we prove that?" Elizabeth asked. "What if Anita doesn't admit to pricing anything?"

"Well, now you're getting into high imaginations," Martha said. "Let's not worry about something that hasn't even happened yet. I know Anita is high strung, but she's always been honest, hasn't she?"

"I—I guess so," Elizabeth said. "Truthfully, I don't really know her that well. She really seemed to like Mama. I don't think she'd purposely do anything to hurt Mama's daughters."

"Like suing us?" Mary asked sarcastically.

Elizabeth sighed. "Like Martha said, let's not worry about what *might* happen. Instead, let's focus on getting everything back. Once we give it all to Anita, we can stop worrying about being sued."

Martha got up and began to prepare supper. Elizabeth finished her list and stared at it. Was Anita's treasure here? Would they be able to retrieve it?

"I think we need to pray," Elizabeth said.

Mary nodded. "You're right. Only God can sort this thing out and help us find a good solution."

Martha stopped her preparations and joined Mary and Elizabeth at the table. They held hands, and together they called out to God.

CHAPTER FIVE

The next morning the sisters were up early and preparing to go to the barn in order to open at ten o'clock. Mary and Martha had baked well into the early morning hours. Elizabeth knew they were tired. She was too, but not because she'd spent time in the kitchen. She'd gone to bed, but instead of sleeping, she'd stared up at the ceiling, trying to sort out their next move. Today they would begin contacting people, asking if they could buy back the items they'd purchased from the Smucker estate. Would it make them look incompetent? How could they make a request without alerting their customers that they might have something more valuable than they realized? Elizabeth knew they needed to be as discreet as possible, but how would they accomplish that? She hated the idea of being dishonest in any way.

She'd finally fallen asleep, but she'd dreamt she was being chased by a Civil War soldier holding a sword made of gold and wearing an emerald-and-diamond bracelet. The dream was so ludicrous, she actually woke up laughing. At least for a while. But concern for the shop and for her sisters quickly chased away any hint of humor in their situation. It wasn't just the financial aspect or the fact that Anita could ruin their reputations. It was knowing that Mary and Martha both needed this venture to work. And truth be told, so did Elizabeth. She didn't want to be alone anymore. If the shop failed and her sisters left, what would happen to her? After Mama died, she'd shut herself in the house, not wanting to go anywhere. Now she had a purpose again. A reason to face the day.

As Elizabeth was just finishing her kitchen clean-up chores, a knock sounded at the back door. Before she could dry her hands and move to answer it, the door opened and Phoebe Fischer, the oldest daughter of Silas and Rachel Fischer, their nearest neighbors to the east, stepped inside, a wicker basket draped over one arm. Dressed in traditional Amish attire, her dark blue dress was covered with a crisp white apron. Her bonnet strings hung, untied, over her shoulders. The young woman set the basket on the edge of the counter and spread her arms wide for a hug. Elizabeth was quick to accommodate Phoebe's unspoken request. Phoebe had been born with Down syndrome and, though twenty years old, she functioned on the approximate age level of an eight-year-old. She had no inhibitions when it came to openly expressing affection.

"So, how are you this morning, Phoebe?" Elizabeth asked. She pulled away from the hug and took Phoebe's hands in hers. "Did Adam's cows provide us lots of good milk, cheese, and butter this week?"

Phoebe nodded, her entire face lighting up in a wide smile. "Oh *ja*, Miss Lizzy," she said. "Have a look." She pulled the linen cloth away from her basket to reveal six glass bottles of fresh milk, a large block of hand-churned butter, and a wheel of cheese, which had been processed by her neighbor's loving hands. Over two years ago now, when Phoebe's older brother, Adam, married, and he and his new bride took up residence in the dawdy haus on his parents' farm, Elizabeth made a handshake agreement to let Adam use the Classens' fallow farmland as pasture for his dairy cows in exchange for a weekly supply of dairy products. She occasionally felt a twinge of guilt, for she was certain she had received the better end of the deal.

"My *maam* says to tell you that she hopes to come by today or tomorrow and see how your shop is coming along." Phoebe's eyes sparkled with excitement, and she added, "And she is bringing a surprise!"

Elizabeth laughed, the heaviness she'd been feeling all morning lifting for a moment. "You tell your mother we'd love to see her, but she really doesn't need to bring us a thing." Phoebe's mother, Rachel, had always been the best neighbor one could hope for, but especially since the passing of Elizabeth's mother, she had become a dear friend.

"Oh, but she does!" Phoebe exclaimed. "We made it just for your store. But I promised not to tell you what it is."

"All right then, Phoebe. Don't you tell me." Elizabeth patted the young woman on the shoulder. "I love surprises." She emptied the basket and put the items in the refrigerator, then handed a wrapped loaf of pumpkin bread to Phoebe. "Here's something sweet to pay you for making the delivery. Now, you be careful going home. I've got to get to work myself." She exchanged another hug with Phoebe before seeing her out the door.

Throughout the morning, Elizabeth couldn't shake the feeling of dread that covered her like a heavy cloak. Yesterday morning she'd been filled with hope, but today she had a hard time seeing any light at the end of the tunnel. She was looking through a stack of books when one of them fell off the table. She picked it up and looked down at the open page. She read:

"For the joy of the LORD is your strength." Nehemiah 8:10.

In Psalm 34, David said, "I will bless the LORD at all times: his praise shall continually be in my mouth" (verse 1). It's easy to praise in the good times, but when we can praise God in the difficult times, it shows where our confidence lies. God is on your side! Trust Him, and He will bring victory to your situation!

Tears sprang to Elizabeth's eyes. She tried to blink them away so she could see to put the devotional book back on the table, but it took several seconds. It was a fair question. Where was her faith? Why had she allowed a temporary setback to cause her so much fear?

"I'm sorry, Lord," she whispered. "I believe opening this store was Your will. You brought my sisters home because we all need each other. I have to put this into Your hands and believe You'll work everything out."

The heavy feeling she'd been fighting all morning suddenly lifted. God hadn't forgotten them at all. He was with them, and He'd see them through.

"Lizzie." Elizabeth turned around to find Mary standing behind her, frowning.

"Is everything okay?"

"I don't know." Mary held up a tablet with a photo of a painting on it. "Do you remember this?"

Elizabeth shook her head. "It doesn't ring a bell with me right now."

"It belonged to Warren Smucker. It's not among our inventory, but I clearly recall seeing it."

Elizabeth stared at her sister. "What are you saying?"

"If our records are correct, we haven't sold it, but it seems to have disappeared."

Elizabeth thought for a moment. "We had some donations that weren't quite ready to be displayed," she said. "I thought everything from the Smucker estate was prepared before the opening, but let me check the inventory room. Maybe it's still there."

Mary nodded at her sister and walked away to help an elderly woman who was looking at a blender.

Elizabeth told Martha where she was going and went to the large room at the back of the barn where they stored inventory. It took her a few minutes to go through everything, but there wasn't any painting like the one Mary had shown her. In fact, there wasn't anything from the Smucker estate. As she looked around, she wondered why Mary had a photo of the painting. Had she snapped a picture of everything that had come from the Smuckers? She hurried back to the shop and found her sister straightening up a large shelf full of bakeware.

"There's no painting like that back there," she said quietly. "Where did you get the picture you showed me?"

Mary crossed her arms and leaned against a nearby table. "I realized I hadn't seen the painting lately, so I searched online by describing the painting."

"Oh, I thought maybe you'd taken pictures of Anita's things."

"Actually, I did. Martha asked me to so she could put the inventory list together. But I didn't get a shot of this painting before it disappeared. After I went online, it didn't take long for me to find what I was looking for. I'm pretty sure this is what it looked like." She pulled the picture up on her tablet once again. Elizabeth looked closely at it. There was a young woman sitting near a window. She was writing a letter. Lying in the girl's lap was a sleeping cat. The colors in the painting were rich and appealing. The light from the window created a deep glow that highlighted the subject's face and touched the rest of the room with gold. "Lizzie, this is a painting by a sixteenth-century painter named Torelli. It was stolen years ago from a museum in Italy." She paused, and her eyes grew wide. "It's worth six million dollars."

Elizabeth had to bite her lip to keep from laughing out loud. "Oh, Mary. What would Warren Smucker be doing with a stolen Italian painting? That mild-mannered little man certainly didn't seem like an international art thief."

Mary scowled at her sister. "But we don't really know, do we?"

"Well, maybe not, but I don't think this painting was among the items Anita brought us. I just don't remember it."

Mary seemed to study her for a moment. "But I do. Do you think I'm lying?"

Elizabeth sighed. "Of course not. But couldn't you be mistaken?"

"No, I'm absolutely certain."

Elizabeth wrapped her arms around herself. The air wasn't cold, but for some reason a chill ran through her. "Then why isn't it on our inventory list?"

Mary shook her head slowly. "Only one reason I can think of. Someone took it before we were able to make a note of it."

"We were the only people near Anita's pieces, and none of us stole it."

"Well, Lizzie, there was one other person...."

Elizabeth thought for a moment. When she realized what Mary was inferring, she shook her head. "Are you saying that Ruth Zook, *our pastor's wife*, took it? That's ridiculous."

"Now, wait a minute. You were a little suspicious about the bracelet. Why don't you think she might have taken the painting?"

"Well, she *bought* the bracelet. Maybe she found out it was worth more than we thought, but the painting... Well, she would have had to *steal* it. As I said before, I'm confident our pastor's wife isn't a thief."

Mary shrugged. "Anita wants to know the location of every-thing we sold. The painting is missing, and we didn't sell it. It's going to be hard to explain what happened to it."

"Yes, it is. We have to follow up on it. We need to figure out where it is."

Mary nodded her agreement. "Yes, we do. I really think this is the item she's looking for, Lizzie."

Elizabeth sighed. "Well, let's hope not. I still say it's not likely." She thought for a moment. "I'll bet, even if it does look like that, it's a print and not the original."

"This wasn't a print, Lizzie. I looked at it myself. I'm a painter, and I know what a real painting looks like."

Elizabeth watched as her sister walked away. Could the picture be the treasure Anita was looking for? Could they re-ally have lost something so valuable? Elizabeth walked back to the table where she'd placed the devotional book she'd dropped earlier, picked it up, and took it to the front of the shop where Martha was checking out customers. She was prob-ably going to need its inspiration a lot in the upcoming days.

She looked up to see Rachel Fischer climbing out of her buggy just outside the open barn doors. Phoebe waved at Elizabeth as she prepared to exit the buggy after her mother. Rachel's twins, Thomas and Matthew, were already kicking dirt at one another as they made their way around the horses toward the shop, their six-year-old sister, Dorcas, trailing behind them. Rachel reached into the back of her buggy and pulled out a large bundle wrapped in brown paper, which Phoebe insisted on carrying. As they approached, Elizabeth called for her sisters to join her in greeting their neighbors. Both Mary and

Martha exchanged hugs with Phoebe and ushered the Fischer family into the store.

"*Guten morgen*, my friends," Rachel said. "It is so good to see these doors open wide and your maam's shop back in business again." She turned to take in the interior filled with items of every kind. "This makes my heart sing."

Elizabeth wished she felt the same way at the moment, but she put on her best smile and tried to shake off her troubles. "Welcome, Rachel. Phoebe told me to expect you. We're so glad to see you here."

"Well, what kind of neighbor would I be if I didn't come to pray God's blessing on your new endeavors?" Rachel laid a gentle hand on Elizabeth's arm, then nodded in greeting to Martha and Mary. "I know you are busy, so we will not stay but a minute. However, we wanted to bless you with a little something to help toward your success." She motioned for Phoebe to offer the package she held to Elizabeth. "Now, this is a gift, and you are to use it as you see fit. However, I was thinking you might want to add it to your merchandise and sell it to help make ends meet. No doubt your expenses have been great as you've prepared to open for business."

Elizabeth couldn't help but think to herself, *She has no idea.* Tears welled in her eyes as she accepted the gift and tore away the paper to reveal an intricately handstitched quilt in an Amish basket pattern. Rachel Fischer was known throughout Lancaster County and beyond for her beautiful quilts. "Oh, Rachel, you really shouldn't have." Mary and Martha echoed her sentiment, and all three of the Classen sisters caressed the soft fabric.

"You would not want to rob us of a blessing, now would you?" Rachel pulled Dorcas by her side and draped her arm over the six-year-old's shoulder as she spoke. The shy girl, her head hidden beneath her bonnet, wrapped herself in her mother's apron. The twins had wandered off to look at a display of old bicycles and toy wagons just outside the barn doors.

"No, of course we wouldn't," Mary said. "But how can we ever say thank you enough? This is much too precious a gift!"

"The gift of God's love, that is too precious." Rachel laughed, then said, "This…this is just a little something I threw together in my spare time." She laughed again.

In unison, Elizabeth, Mary, and Martha shook their heads and added their laughter to Rachel's. They all knew that their Amish neighbor poured hours and hours of loving care into each quilt she made. "We will display it prominently," Mary said. "But I, for one, just might secretly wish it doesn't sell too soon, so we can enjoy its beauty for many days to come."

"I second that wish," Martha said.

"And I third it!" Elizabeth pulled Phoebe into another hug. "Thank you all. We are truly blessed to have you as neighbors and as friends." As she spoke the words, she offered up a silent prayer of thanksgiving for God's reminders that, even in the midst of trouble, they were not alone.

CHAPTER SIX

The next morning Mary and Martha offered to run the store while Elizabeth made phone calls, trying to retrieve everything that had been sold from the Smucker estate. She thought about asking Anita if they could ignore a few items—like some embroidered pillowcases and several cast-iron skillets—but in the end, Elizabeth decided to follow her instructions to the letter. The pillowcases and skillets had been sold to Esther Vogel, a lovely Amish woman who lived on a farm a few miles out of town. Elizabeth planned to save her for last since she couldn't call her. She dreaded asking Esther to return things that couldn't possibly be valuable.

Taking a deep breath, she began making her calls. Thankfully, most people were very understanding, if a bit confused. Elizabeth didn't go into any long explanations; she just told them that Anita had changed her mind and had decided she wasn't ready to sell anything right now. Most people took that to mean that she was struggling with her father's death, and they were very compassionate. But there were a few holdouts.

"Now why in the world would Anita Smucker care if I have her mama's old sewing machine?" Mabel Trundle asked. "Her mama died ten years ago, and this thing sat there, unused, ever since she passed. I don't get it."

"How do you know it was unused?" Elizabeth said, trying to stay calm. "Maybe Anita wants to sew something with it."

"I don't think so." Mabel sniffed. "It took me thirty minutes to oil and loosen the gears so the poor thing would work. Is she going to pay me for my time?"

"I don't know, Mabel. I can ask her."

Elizabeth listened to a little grumbling before Mabel finally said, "I'll drop it off at your place."

Elizabeth quickly thanked her and hung up. She wasn't worried about most of the calls she had to make, but she didn't know what to do about Uriah Barnhart and Ruth Zook. Although Uriah wasn't Amish, it appeared as though he didn't have a phone. Or, if he did, the number wasn't one she could find.

Elizabeth worked until lunchtime and then left the house to check on her sisters. Martha pulled her aside as she walked into the old barn.

"We're doing fine, but people are beginning to talk about our request to return things from the Smuckers."

"I assumed it wouldn't take long," Elizabeth replied. "Has anything been brought back this morning?"

Martha nodded. "Several items. I've got them in the back. If you want to stay here and help Mary for a few minutes, I'll take them into the house."

"Sure. Go ahead."

Elizabeth sat down near the front register and waited for customers to bring her their purchases. She'd only been there a few minutes when the door opened and Mabel came in, carrying the sewing machine. She plopped it down on the table where Elizabeth sat, and Elizabeth heard something snap from under the tabletop. The old wooden table wasn't in very good shape. It wouldn't hold up under the weight of too many sewing machines being dropped on it.

"There you go," Mabel said huffily. "That'll be thirty bucks."

Elizabeth opened the register and counted out the money. Although she was certain Mabel had paid less than that, it wasn't the time to argue. Mabel grabbed her money and stormed out, almost running into Billy Richmond, who had just stepped inside the barn.

"Wow, she was in a hurry," he said to Elizabeth.

"It's a long story. Not one I feel like talking about right now. I'm sorry."

Billy nodded. "I understand. Not sure I even want to hear it." He crooked his head toward the front door. "I wonder if you'd step out here for just a minute. I have something that might make things easier for you."

Elizabeth frowned at him, not sure what he was talking about.

"What's going on?" Mary walked up to the table after helping a customer.

"Billy has something outside he wants to show us," she told Mary.

Elizabeth got up and walked out the door with Mary on her heels. What she saw stunned her. It was a long, L-shaped counter. Fashioned in rich oak, polished and beautiful, it was breathtaking.

"I...I don't understand," Elizabeth said. "What is this?"

When Billy smiled at her, Elizabeth noticed his face flushed a little. He was obviously embarrassed by the attention.

"I noticed you were using an old rickety table for your register, and I wasn't at all sure it would hold up much longer. Thought maybe you needed something sturdier."

Elizabeth's mouth dropped open at the timing, since she'd just been wondering how long their old table would last.

"But...but how did you find the time to make this?" Mary asked, running her hand over the smooth countertop.

"I started it back when we first began renovations. You told me about your plans to use a table at the front of the store. Figured you'd be happier with something like this."

Elizabeth was dumbstruck. "What do we owe you?" she asked, hoping it wasn't too expensive. With the Smucker situation, money wasn't abundant.

"Owe me?" Billy shook his head. "I'd never build something without your permission and ask you to pay for it."

Immediately, Elizabeth felt bad about her question. Before she could respond, Mary walked up next to him.

"My sister is very practical, Billy. She doesn't mean anything by what she said. She just doesn't want to take advantage of your kindness."

Mary's words made Billy's smile return. He swung his gaze from Mary back to Elizabeth. "It's a gift. I really want to see you all succeed. Down through the years, your dad and mom were very kind to me." He looked down at the ground, obviously trying to rein in his emotions. "This is the least I could do for them...and their daughters."

"You've already done so much, Billy," Elizabeth said, her voice shaking with emotion. "I don't know what I would have done without you before Mama died. You were always there for us."

"Just trying to give back what was given to me."

Mary reached out and put her hand on his arm. "Thank you, Billy. We receive it…with gratitude. It's so beautiful."

"Yes, Billy," Elizabeth echoed. "Thank you. I honestly don't know what to say."

"And for my sister, that's highly unusual," Mary said, laughing.

Billy chuckled. Elizabeth noticed his expression as he gazed at Mary. He was clearly smitten.

"How did you get this here?" Mary asked.

Billy cocked his head toward his truck. "My friend Ernest came with me. If you like it and want it inside, we'll move it in for you."

Elizabeth and Mary said "Yes!" at the same time, causing all of them to laugh.

Billy headed over to his truck and spoke to Ernest, who was sitting in the passenger seat. He got out and came over to where the counter sat on the ground. Billy and Ernest picked it up, straining under the weight. The men carried it inside the barn while Elizabeth and Mary quickly removed their cash register and pulled the old table out of the way. The counter fit perfectly in the space they had.

Martha, who'd been straightening shelves, came jogging up to them. "What in the world…?"

Elizabeth quickly explained the wonderful gift to her sister.

"It's beautiful," Martha said softly. She smiled at Billy. "Thank you. My mother would approve."

Billy nodded. "That means a lot. Your mama was a wonderful person."

"Yes, she was."

Out of the corner of her eye, Elizabeth saw a woman looking at kitchen appliances who appeared to need help. She grabbed Martha's hand and pulled her sister a few yards away from the couple.

"What are you doing?" Martha asked, wrenching her hand out of her sister's.

"I'm *trying* to give Billy and Mary some time alone. I assume you approve. She's got to start meeting men who aren't anything like Brian."

Martha sighed. "Of course I approve. But next time you might give me a heads-up before you kidnap me."

"Well, it's hardly kidnapping. I mean..."

"I'm just teasing you, Lizzie. Relax." She noticed the same woman Elizabeth had. "Let me help that customer. Then I'd like a lunch break, if it's okay."

Elizabeth nodded. "Sure, but you might need to keep it short. I've got to go out this afternoon."

Martha frowned at her. "Is this about Anita's stuff?"

Elizabeth nodded. "I guess I'm going to need to pay personal visits to Uriah Barnhart and Ruth Zook. Uriah doesn't have a phone, and I feel I need to talk to Ruth in person."

"I don't envy you. With either one of them. Uriah's a little scary and Ruth... Well, I still don't believe she took that painting."

"I don't either."

"How are you going to approach her?"

Elizabeth sighed and clasped her hands together. "I don't know. I'll bring up the bracelet… And then I guess I'll just ask her if she remembers the painting. Tell her we've lost it somehow. I certainly have no intention of accusing her of anything."

"Do you want me to go with you?"

"I wish you could," Elizabeth said. "But I don't want to leave Mary by herself."

Martha nodded toward their younger sister, who was still talking to Billy. "Maybe Billy could help somehow."

Elizabeth put her arms around Martha and gave her a quick hug. "I'm sure he'd be willing to do anything we asked, but this is something we need to take care of ourselves. Besides, I don't want to push things too fast between Mary and Billy. She still seems pretty fragile in the area of romance, no matter how slow a relationship might progress right now." She let go of her sister and studied Billy and Mary for a moment.

"He is a good man though, isn't he, Sis?" Martha asked softly.

Elizabeth smiled. "I believe he is. I just don't know if Mary will allow him—or anyone—to get close. You're right. She has pretty deep scars from Brian."

"I know." Martha shook her head. "I'd like to punch him in the nose."

Elizabeth grinned at her. "Not very *Mennonite* of you, Sister."

"When it comes to my family being mistreated, I don't *feel* very Mennonite. I feel like a mother tiger protecting her young."

Elizabeth grabbed her hand. "You don't have to protect us. Besides, you're still healing yourself. Have I ever told you how much I respect you?"

"No, not lately."

Elizabeth smiled. "Well, I do, you know. And I love you too."

Martha chuckled. "Good combination. I'll take it." Her expression turned serious. "I'll keep my cell phone close. If you need help this afternoon, you call me, okay?"

Elizabeth snorted. "I'll be fine. I think I can take on an old man and a pastor's wife if I have to."

Martha laughed and walked away. Although Elizabeth had made light of the awkward visits in front of her this afternoon, her stomach churned nervously. She didn't enjoy confrontation and prayed she could do what had to be done without creating enemies in her community.

CHAPTER SEVEN

E xcuse me."

Mary turned around to find a middle-aged woman standing behind her.

"Can I help you?" Mary asked.

"I hope so," the woman said. "Do you have pictures?"

"Pictures? What kind of pictures?"

The woman looked at her as if she were dense. "You know, pictures. Paintings. Like you put on the wall."

"Oh, certainly. Yes, we do. If you'll follow me, I'd be happy to help you."

The woman stayed behind her as Mary led the way to the far side of the barn. She and her sisters had created an area specifically for large pictures and paintings. They had some that were perfect for a child's room, while others were more suited for living room walls. Another section had cute wall hangings for kitchens. There were a couple of real paintings, but the sisters wondered if they'd sell. Their mother hadn't carried them because she'd said most painters expected top dollar for their work. In a shop like theirs, most customers were looking for bargains. However, the sisters hoped that tourists who came to Lancaster County might be interested in local art as well. Time would tell. Mary hoped their gamble would pay off. She'd love to display some of her own work, but the idea that her paintings would just sit and gather dust didn't appeal to her in the least.

Mary stopped in front of the wall covered with pictures. "Maybe you'll see something here you like."

As the woman scanned the display, her expression became tight, and her mouth turned into a thin line. Finally she whirled around and scowled at Mary. "It's not here. Where is it?"

Mary was so startled by the woman's reaction she couldn't think of a response. That seemed to incense the woman even more, and she pointed her finger in Mary's face.

"You know the one I want. The picture of the girl and the cat. Where is it?"

"The girl and the cat?" Mary asked slowly. "You mean the Torelli?" She studied the woman carefully. What did she know about the missing painting?

"I don't know the name of the painter. I just know it's a girl and a cat, and I want it. Are you going to tell me where it is?"

"Who told you we had it?"

The woman looked away from her, as if scouting out the barn to make sure no one was listening. "You don't need to know that. I just want the painting. Please. I have to have it."

Mary thought quickly. She'd never seen the woman before, but it was obvious she knew something about the missing painting. Mary decided to change tactics. She smiled at the woman, who was obviously getting more nervous by the moment. "I'll tell you what. Let me get your name and number. I know the painting you're talking about. It might still be in storage. As soon as I locate it, I'll call you."

For a few seconds, Mary thought her tactic had worked. The woman seemed to consider her request. Then as suddenly as she'd mellowed, she was angry again. She stepped up to within a few inches of Mary's face. Although her first reaction was to pull away, Mary stood her ground.

"I've got to have that painting, and I'll do whatever I must to get it," the woman hissed. With that, she stomped out, leaving Mary stunned. The shock of the woman's threat caused her to freeze momentarily. When she realized she should try to get the woman's license plate number, she ran toward the front of the store. As she jogged past, Martha looked at her as if she were crazy, but Mary didn't have time to explain.

When she pushed the front door open, she saw a black car racing out of their parking lot, headed for the road. Not knowing what else to do, Mary jumped into her car, planning to follow the woman's vehicle. As she started the engine, she reached into her purse and pulled out her phone. If she could just get close enough to snap a picture of the license plate, maybe the police could figure out who the woman was. From there perhaps they could find out the truth about the painting. This woman seemed to have information about it. Mary was almost to the road when, suddenly, a buggy pulled in front of her, effectively blocking her way. She slammed on her brakes and stopped within a few feet of the buggy carrying an Amish couple and their two children. They stared at Mary with alarm clearly written on their faces. Mary got out of her car and apologized for driving too fast, feeling awful. People around Bird-in-Hand were especially considerate of their Amish neighbors. A terrible accident not far from town several years ago still had everyone on edge.

The Amish couple smiled at her graciously and flicked their reins, continuing down the road. Mary got back in her car and waited until they were well clear. Then she turned toward the direction the woman had driven, but it was too late. After traveling a few miles, she couldn't find the car again. Sighing with frustration, she turned around and drove back to the shop.

What was it about this painting? And where was it? Mary couldn't wait for Elizabeth to get back, so she could tell her what had happened. But for now, she needed to explain her wild behavior to Martha.

It took Elizabeth some time to find Uriah's house. She'd driven by it before and thought she knew where it was, but she wasn't great with directions. As she circled a block that she was sure she'd been around at least twice, she finally spotted it. Actually, his home was easy to pick out. It was a huge Victorian in desperate need of paint and attention. The house had been in disrepair before Uriah left, but while he was gone, conditions only worsened. An old wrought iron fence surrounded the property, but many of the decorative railings were either missing or broken. Elizabeth suspected that neighborhood teenagers had busted the fence for the fun of it. The gate hung halfway off, and the yard was overgrown with weeds. If there had ever been grass on the lawn, it had been choked out years ago.

Elizabeth parked her car and walked up the stone sidewalk to the front porch. There were broken boards on the floor of the porch, and she carefully stepped around them, hoping her foot wouldn't go through the wood and make a new hole. She knocked gingerly on the dilapidated front door, really hoping no one would answer.

After several seconds of silence, Elizabeth heard some odd noises from the other side, a rustling sound, and then, suddenly, the doorknob rattled. Finally, the door opened slowly, creaking so loudly, Elizabeth wanted to cover her ears. A wrinkled, wizened face peered at her through the torn screen door. Uriah's expression reminded Elizabeth of an angry troll.

"What do you want?" Uriah asked, staring at her suspiciously, his eyes narrowed into slits.

"Hello, Mr. Barnhart. I'm Elizabeth Classen. You know, from Secondhand Blessings?"

"Secondhand...what? Is this some kind of church? I'm not interested."

He started to close the door. Elizabeth knew she wouldn't have the guts to go through all this a second time, so she quickly said, "No, Mr. Barnhart. I'm not from a church. You bought a sword from us the other day? A Civil War sword?"

"So? You want more money for it? I won't give you another dime. Now get out of here."

Elizabeth thought quickly. "No, Mr. Barnhart. I don't want more money. I want to give *you* some money."

That made a difference. Uriah pushed the door open the rest of the way, the creak setting Elizabeth's teeth on edge. "Come in," he barked.

Elizabeth stepped past him, unsure of what she might find in a hermit's home. The living room furniture was old and threadbare, but the space was neat. It was obvious the room had been beautiful and elegant at one time. What had happened that he'd let it go to pot like this?

"I guess you can sit down there," Uriah said, pointing at the couch.

Elizabeth quickly scanned the brocade couch, making sure it was clean. It looked fine except for a spring that poked out from the cushion near one of the arms. She quickly sat down on the other side.

"So I'll ask you again. What do you want? Why do you want to give me money?"

Uriah's angry stare made her gulp a couple of times. With effort, she cleared her throat. "I'm truly sorry to bother you with this, Mr. Barnhart, but as I said, I must talk to you about the sword we sold you."

Uriah's forehead furrowed, and he raised one eyebrow. His other eye disappeared under an avalanche of wrinkled skin. "I bought that sword fair and square."

"I know that, Mr. Barnhart. I'm not saying you didn't. But there's a problem. The original owner has changed her mind about selling it. I'm here to buy it back from you. I'll give you the full amount you paid."

Although Elizabeth expected her news to irritate the old man, it seemed to have an opposite effect. The corners of his mouth turned up, and his eyes widened with surprise. "She wants it back? Seriously?" He threw his head back and laughed, but it wasn't a pleasant sound. Then he shook his head and pointed his finger at Elizabeth. "You tell Anita Smucker that it will be a cold day in…you know where…before she sees that sword again. And she knows why!" He walked over to the door and swung it open. "I don't blame you for coming here, Miss Classen, but I have no intention of giving you my sword."

"But Mr. Barnhart, surely you can understand why she's changed her mind. I mean, after her dad's death and all…."

The odd little man rocked back on his heels and smiled strangely at Elizabeth. "She doesn't want that sword returned because it belonged to her father. She wants it back because she finally understands what the sword really means."

Elizabeth frowned at him. "What it means? I don't understand—"

"The real reason she's trying to get it back?" Uriah snapped. "Well, that's for me to know and for you to find out. I'll thank you to get off my property now."

Not knowing what else to do, Elizabeth stood. "Perhaps you could tell me just how much it would take for you to part with the sword. I can pass the information along to Anita…"

Uriah took a step toward her, and Elizabeth shrank back. "You tell her there's no amount of money in this world that will buy back that sword." He pointed toward the door. "I'm trying to be as nice as I can to you, Miss Classen. Because of your mama. She was always kind to me. But Warren Smucker is through pushing me around. I won't give back what's mine, no matter what the rest of his family says or does. Now, you need to leave."

Elizabeth couldn't think of anything else to say, so she turned around and headed for the front door. As she passed by an entrance that led to another room, she noticed an antique buffet with something lying on the top. She was pretty sure it was the sword, but she couldn't be sure. She wanted to ask, but since there was no way to reason with Uriah, she stayed silent.

When she stepped out on the front porch, the door slammed shut behind her with an earsplitting creak, causing her to jump. Elizabeth stood there for a few moments trying to figure out what to do next. There was nothing left but to tell Anita she couldn't retrieve the sword. Obviously, Uriah had a past with Warren Smucker, and whatever had happened between them had something to do with that sword. Could it be the item of value Warren had alluded to?

CHAPTER EIGHT

Elizabeth decided to visit Ruth Zook the next day. Her meeting with Uriah had taken everything out of her. Although she couldn't believe Ruth would purposely buy something valuable from them without telling them of its true worth, she just couldn't face any further conflict today.

Instead, she went to see Esther Vogel. Getting back the skillets and pillowcases was so easy, it made Elizabeth feel guilty. She told Esther she would bring her some replacements from the store's inventory that were better than what she was giving up. At first Esther refused, not wanting to cause the Classens to lose money. However, after some gentle prodding, she finally agreed. By the time Elizabeth left, her spirits were somewhat buoyed. As she headed home, she couldn't stop thinking about Uriah's odd reaction to her request to buy the sword back. What was going on? As least it was out of her hands now. She'd tell Anita what Uriah said. After that, it was up to her to talk to him. Elizabeth certainly had no intention of going back there again. Ever.

Martha closed up the shop, and then she and Mary began cleaning up. Once their shelves were straightened and the cashbox secured, the sisters locked up and headed into the house. Mary had already told Martha about the strange woman looking for the missing painting.

"There's something odd about that painting," Martha said. "We really need to figure out what happened to it."

"And we've got to tell Anita it's missing. I don't relish that. She's going to go ballistic."

"Maybe, but unless it suddenly turns up, we don't have a choice."

"So how did we do today?" Mary asked, changing the subject. She plopped herself down at the kitchen table.

Martha shrugged. "I'm not sure. Between people bringing items back and the refunds we issued, I'm not sure we made any money at all."

Mary frowned. "I sold several things that had nothing to do with the Smuckers."

"Let's not talk about it now," Martha said. Sometimes trying to explain finances to Mary was an exercise in futility.

Mary shrugged. "Fine with me."

Martha put the cashbox on the table and sat down next to it. "I'll count everything after supper. Right now, I'm tired and hungry. What would you like for dinner?"

Mary shrugged again. "I don't care. But no more goulash, okay? You know I don't like it."

Martha frowned. "You told Mama you love goulash."

"Sure, because I didn't want to hurt her feelings. But now that she's gone, I'd really rather not have to choke it down."

Martha pushed back the flash of resentment that flared up toward her sister. She loved her mother's goulash, and she made it using her mother's recipe. Not liking it almost felt like betrayal. Of course, that was silly. She took a deep breath and forced herself to think about something else. Something that wouldn't make her feel so indignant.

"Billy's gift was incredible," she said, forcing herself to smile at her sister. "Hard to believe he worked so hard to bless us like that."

Mary nodded. "He's a very nice man. We're fortunate to have him in our lives."

Martha stared at her sister for a moment, trying to decide if she should say anything more about Billy. Finally, she said, "He likes you, you know."

Mary stared down at her clasped hands. "I know," she said quietly. "And I think I could really like him too. But I'm simply not ready..."

Martha reached over and put her hand on Mary's arm. "Honey, not every man is Brian. Chuck was a wonderful person. He always made me feel special. As if I were the only woman in the world. I want that for you someday."

Mary looked up with tears in her eyes. "Don't you think I want that too?" She shook her head. "Until about a month before he left, I had no clue anything was wrong. I thought we were happy. True, we'd settled into a comfortable routine, but we enjoyed being together. Going out. Having fun. By the time I noticed he was acting strangely, it was already too late." A tear ran down her cheek. "What if it happens again? Do you know how it feels to have someone you love look at you as if they don't know you? Brian's expression when he told me he was in love with...her... I'll never forget it. Cold. A stranger's face. Not the face of the man I woke up next to for over twenty years."

Martha tried to swallow past the lump in her throat. Thank the Lord, Chuck had never looked at her like that. If he had... Well, she couldn't imagine it. "Brian's an idiot, Mary. Sometimes men get scared. Afraid they're growing old. What's-her-name made him feel younger. One day he'll realize what a mistake he's made. What he traded away. But by then, I want you to be with someone who makes you happy. Really happy."

Mary grunted. "Can't I be happy without a man in my life?"

"Of course you can, if that's what you want. And if you want to stay single, I'll support you. But if you don't want that for your life, I'll continue to pray that God will heal your broken heart and give you the courage to love again."

Mary squeezed Martha's hand. "Thank you. I do worry about the kids. They don't understand. And they don't want to see their father."

"They will, eventually. They're hurt too, Sis. I'm sure they feel rejected—and they worry about you too."

"I know. Bless their hearts. I don't know what I'd do without them. They've been so supportive."

"Good." Martha pulled her hand back and got up to start supper. "Are they coming to visit soon?"

"Yes, as soon as they can. Michael plans to take vacation time, and Jennifer will be out of school for the summer in a little over a month. They're coming out together."

Martha smiled. "I can hardly wait to see them."

"Me too. They love the store and were so happy to hear we were starting it back up."

Martha laughed. "I still remember Jennifer sneaking her brother's toys onto Mama's shelves and trying to sell them behind his back."

Mary giggled. "Michael wasn't amused."

"No, he wasn't."

The fun memory from the past lightened the mood a little. Martha was grateful for it. With everything they were dealing with, any chance to feel normal was welcome.

Mary got up from the table and opened a drawer in the kitchen. She took out a piece of paper and then sat down again.

"I've been going over Warren Smucker's riddle."

"So read it to me again," Martha said, sighing. "Maybe we can solve the riddle and figure out just what the treasure really is."

"Okay, here goes."

When lightning speaks and feathers fly,
And your mother's sister's child makes dirty pies,
You'll find yourself feeling quite continental.
Open your eyes, and you'll see the truth.
Hidden in shadows and very sentimental.

Martha whispered the words back to herself. What could they mean? "Well, when lightning speaks, it's called thunder, right?"

Mary nodded and wrote something down on the piece of paper. "Sound good to me. But what does *feathers fly* mean?"

Martha sighed. "I have no idea. People say that feathers fly when there's an argument."

"Feathers fly when a feather pillow breaks open."

Martha turned the words over in her head, but nothing she came up with made sense. "Okay, so what's the next line?"

"*And your mother's sister's child makes dirty pies.*"

"Who is your mother's sister's child?"

"Easy," Mary said. "It's your cousin."

Martha considered Mary's suggestion. "That sounds right. So we have *thunder* and *cousin*." She frowned. "Anything in the missing painting that connects to these words?"

"No, not that I can think of."

Martha nodded. "Finish rereading the riddle."

"*You'll find yourself feeling quite continental.*
Open your eyes and you'll see the truth.
Hidden in shadows and very sentimental."

"I don't get it," Martha said. She sighed loudly. "I hate riddles. Always have. They're so frustrating."

"I don't mind them," Mary said. "But I have to say that this one's getting on my nerves."

"We'll work on it more after supper. Why don't you help me with the table? Elizabeth will be home soon. I have a feeling her day wasn't easy."

Mary put the paper back in the drawer. Then she started setting the table.

As she worked, Martha couldn't get the riddle out of her head. What did it mean? Could it help them to find the Smucker treasure, or was it just another rabbit hole going nowhere?

CHAPTER NINE

When Elizabeth got home she was happy to find supper waiting on her. She'd gone by the store, so it was later than usual. A light rain had turned to a chilly drizzle. Since it was early spring, she never knew what to wear when she went out. Thankfully, she'd taken a sweater with her, but still, getting inside where it was warm and sitting down to one of Martha's delicious suppers sounded great. Martha wasn't just a talented baker; she was an overall great cook. Tonight she'd fixed pork chops with fried potatoes and homemade applesauce.

The sisters talked over the events of the day as they ate. Elizabeth expressed concern about the woman who'd been looking for the painting.

"I can't believe that's the stolen painting," Elizabeth said. "It doesn't make sense. What would Warren Smucker be doing with a stolen painting? He always seemed like an honorable man."

"I have no idea," Martha said, "but we need to find out who this woman is. I don't trust her."

"I agree," Mary said. "She seemed...almost desperate."

Elizabeth sighed. "We've also got to tell Anita about the painting. Obviously someone took it. She's not going to be happy."

"There's not much we can do about that," Mary said. "I still can't understand how someone took it without us knowing."

Martha nodded in agreement. "Just add this to the list of things that don't make sense."

From there, the conversation turned to the gift Billy had given them. "We must do something to thank him," Elizabeth said.

"What a great idea, Lizzie," Mary said with enthusiasm. "What shall we do? Invite him to dinner?"

"Why not?" Elizabeth asked. "Dinner, dessert... Something really nice. What about a thank-you gift?"

Martha frowned at her sister. "What kind of gift?"

"Well, we still have Daddy's tools in the basement..."

Mary gasped. "Oh no, Lizzie. We can't give Daddy's tools away."

"We never use them, Mary," Elizabeth said. "We have the basic tools we need in the kitchen drawer. Anything big comes along, we always call Billy. Daddy's tools have been downstairs ever since he passed away. What good are they doing? Someone like Billy could really use them."

"Billy has his own tools, Lizzie," Martha said. "I'm not sure he'd care anything about those old things."

"I don't know," Elizabeth said. "Billy grew up without a father. Daddy was a role model for him. Daddy taught him how to fix stuff—how to craft things from wood. Even if the tools are old, I think they'd mean a lot to Billy because they were Daddy's."

The sisters considered Elizabeth's words in silence. Finally Mary spoke, her voice so low it was hard to hear her. "I think giving the tools to Billy would make Daddy very happy. He loved us, but he always wanted a son too. Billy kind of filled that role."

"You're right," Martha said. Her words were crisp and firm. "We must offer him the tools."

The sisters looked at one another and smiled.

"It's settled then," Elizabeth said. "We'll ask him over Friday evening. And we'll tell him to choose the tools he'd like."

"Agreed," Mary said. "Boy, it sure will feel strange to see Daddy's tools leave this house."

Elizabeth nodded. "But I think we'll all be relieved to know they'll be used again instead of just gathering dust in the basement."

At that moment, Butterscotch yowled loudly, startling Elizabeth.

"I think it's time to feed our menagerie," Martha said. Tinkerbelle yipped at her suggestion, and Elizabeth laughed.

"Let's finish eating, clean up our supper dishes, feed these guys, and take our tea into the living room. I want to tell you about my day."

"I've wanted to ask you," Martha said, "but I'm a little afraid to find out the results. Was Ruth upset?"

"I didn't visit Ruth today. That's on my schedule for tomorrow. Today I talked to Esther and to Uriah Barnhart. *That* conversation was very interesting."

"I can only imagine," Martha said. "He seems like a strange bird."

Elizabeth sighed. "You have no idea."

After clearing up the supper dishes and feeding assorted pets, the sisters gathered in the living room with tea and cookies. Elizabeth and Martha drank decaf while Mary took hers with caffeine. She never seemed to have a problem sleeping, something Elizabeth assumed would change as she got older.

She told them about her meeting with Uriah, trying to not leave anything out.

"Then the sword must be the treasure," Mary said. "It has to be."

"I don't know," Elizabeth said, "but there's certainly something strange going on. Uriah acted as if the sword was his and that Anita shouldn't have had it. He also made it sound as if Anita knew something about it that we don't."

Martha frowned. "But if there's some kind of special story behind the sword, Anita would probably know about it, right? I mean, she would probably be aware of its value. That would mean it couldn't be what she's looking for."

Elizabeth shrugged. "That makes sense, but I'm just not sure. I'd really like to know more about its history. Maybe..."

Elizabeth stopped talking when a loud banging sound came from outside. She looked at Mary and Martha. "What in the world..."

Pal, who had been let outside earlier, began barking wildly. Elizabeth got up and hurried toward the door.

"Lizzie, wait!" Mary called out. "What if someone's out there?"

Exasperated, Elizabeth turned and scowled at her sister. "That's why I'm going outside."

"It might be dangerous."

"What would you like me to do? Ignore the situation and hope it goes away?"

Martha ran over and opened an antique cabinet in the corner of the living room. Inside was their father's old hunting rifle. She grabbed it and joined her sister at the door.

"That thing's not loaded," Elizabeth snapped. "Besides, it's so old I doubt it would work even if it were."

"Well, whoever's out there doesn't know that."

Elizabeth rolled her eyes. "Oh boy. It's probably Bossy again. She's strayed from the pasture and come to pay a visit several times since my arrangement with Adam."

"I'm taking it, Lizzie, and I don't want to argue about it."

Frustrated, Elizabeth decided to give in. When Martha got an idea in her head, there was no talking her out of it. "Fine. You bring that useless rifle. I'll get a flashlight, if you don't mind." She opened up a cabinet door and pulled out a flashlight, which she held in front of her like a weapon. When she turned around, she noticed Tinkerbelle cowering under the table. "Lots of help you are," she said.

Then, with her sisters on her heels, Elizabeth slowly opened the front door. The porch light was on, which actually made it harder to see the barn and easier for anyone outside to see them. Even so, she just couldn't turn it off. The sun had just gone down, and even with the flashlight it was difficult to see anything. There was an outside light on the barn, but they'd have to be inside the barn to turn it on.

The three women had just stepped outside when something jumped up on the porch. Mary screamed, and Pal sat down in front of them with a look of confusion on his face.

Mary leaned down and ran her hand over his head. "I'm sorry, boy. You scared me."

Elizabeth called the border collie over to her. "You stay with us," she said. Pal was a great dog, but following instructions wasn't one of his strongest qualities. He immediately began to run toward the barn, barking incessantly. Then he took off around the side of the building, and they lost sight of him. Elizabeth wondered why he hadn't barked earlier if someone really was on their property. Chances were he'd only just arrived home. Every evening he liked to visit the horses at the Fischers' farm.

"Pal! Pal, get back here," Martha hissed. She shook her head and grabbed Elizabeth's arm. "He's going to scare the intruder away."

"And that's a bad thing?" Mary asked. "Were you looking forward to meeting him?"

"I'd like to catch him," she said emphatically, holding the gun in front of her. She gave Mary an incredulous glare. "You want him to get away?"

Mary's head bounced up and down like a bobble head doll. "Yeah, as far as possible."

Martha sighed dramatically. "My sister, the wimp."

"Your sister—who wants to live."

"Both of you hush," Elizabeth said. "We're not exactly stealthy. Whoever was out there is probably at home and having supper by now. We still haven't even made it off this porch."

Martha sighed and walked down the steps, swinging the rifle around as if she were ready to shoot anything that moved. She gazed to the east, toward the Fischers' farm. Mary and

Elizabeth followed behind her, and Elizabeth followed Martha's gaze. She hoped it really was Adam Fischer's cow. Bossy and Pal were friends. Pal had stopped barking, which made her wonder if they really were tracking Bossy.

As the sisters approached the door of the barn, Pal came running from around the side of the building. He seemed pretty happy with himself and deposited something on the ground. Elizabeth shone the flashlight on it as Mary bent down and picked it up. It was a piece of blue fabric with small flowers. Mary held it up, and Elizabeth moved closer, peering at it. Its ragged edges made it clear it had been torn off something.

"Do you think Pal bit someone?" Mary asked.

"I don't know. There's no blood on the material, and I've never known him to attack anyone."

Mary frowned. "Don't think I'm crazy, but this looks familiar. I just can't place it."

"It's pretty small, Mary," Martha said.

Elizabeth stuck the scrap of fabric in her pocket. "Well, right now it's the only evidence we have." She pulled a key out of her other pocket and slid it into the lock on the door. She was surprised to find it was already unlocked. Frowning, she slowly swung the large door open.

"Let me go in first," Martha ordered. She stepped around Elizabeth with her rifle pointing inside the barn, still acting as if the gun she held in her hands was a real threat.

Elizabeth snorted. "What are you going to do if we actually confront someone? Pull the trigger and yell 'bang!' as loud as you can?"

"Shh," Mary interjected. "For Pete's sake, Lizzie. You don't tell the bad guys your gun doesn't work."

Elizabeth sighed and rolled her eyes. This was turning into a scene from the *Three Stooges*. She flipped the inside light on as well as the outside light. Illumination made it clear that the problem wasn't Bossy. One of the windows on the side of the barn was broken, and a large table near the front door was on its side. Some of the shelves had been toppled, and items were scattered everywhere. Secondhand Blessings had been robbed!

CHAPTER TEN

O h my," Mary said in a frightened whisper. "Maybe the thieves are still inside. We should—"

"Look." Elizabeth pointed at Pal, who waited calmly next to them. "If anyone was here, we'd know it. Whoever broke in is gone now."

Martha put the rifle down on a nearby table. "This place is a mess." She pointed at her sisters. "Don't touch anything. I'll call the police."

"I doubt seriously if the police are going to dust for finger-prints in a secondhand store," Elizabeth said. "This isn't like those crime shows you like to watch."

"Humor me," Martha said firmly. "Leave everything alone until the police say it's okay."

Mary let out a deep breath. "Fine, but we'll be here all night cleaning up. How are we going to open tomorrow?"

As Martha left to get her phone, Elizabeth put her arm around Mary. "We'll do the best we can. Maybe we can move some of this for now..." Elizabeth let go of her younger sister. "The back. I didn't think to check..."

The two women hurried to the back of the barn where items that hadn't been added into the inventory were stored. Sure enough, the thieves had been there as well. Many things were knocked over and thrown around.

"Oh dear," Mary said. "This lamp is broken and so is this beautiful mirror."

"We're going to have to pay for everything that's ruined," Elizabeth said, trying not to get emotional. "We're talking hundreds of dollars."

"We have insurance, right?"

"Sure, but there's a high deductible."

Mary and Elizabeth stared at each other for a minute. "Why would someone do this? There's nothing that valuable in here," Mary said, her voice breaking.

Although Elizabeth, too, felt like sitting down and having a good cry, she said instead, "Everything will be all right. We'll put in a claim and see what the insurance pays. And we'll take whatever we need to out of our savings." She smiled at her sister. "We'll be up and running again in no time."

Mary seemed to find some solace in Elizabeth's assurances and went off to find out what was missing or destroyed. Elizabeth surveyed the large room. Although she hadn't memorized everything in the shop, she had pretty good recall. So far she hadn't noticed anything missing. It seemed that whoever broke in didn't come just to steal from them. They were obviously looking for something in particular. But what? Did someone else know about Anita's treasure? Could they possibly know what it was? "Don't be silly," she said to herself. "If Anita can't figure it out, how could anyone else know?"

But as she carefully considered her question, she realized it was possible. Where did Warren get his so-called valuable piece? If he'd purchased it, whoever sold it to him would know the value. Did they suspect that Anita might not have any idea how much the piece, whatever it might be, was worth? People in town knew she was trying to collect all the items she'd placed at Secondhand Blessings. Would the original owner conclude it had something to do with the object he'd sold to Warren? Would he try to retrieve it?

Ignoring Martha's advice, Elizabeth began picking up items that had been knocked over, setting them upright, making sure they weren't damaged, and moving the broken lamp and mirror to the side. She used her flashlight to look carefully on the ground in case the person responsible had dropped something that might lead to their identification. When she couldn't find anything, she straightened up and sighed. "Heavens to Betsy," she said softly. "This isn't *Murder, She Wrote,* and you certainly aren't Jessica Fletcher." The series was one of Elizabeth's all-time favorite shows. Where was Jessica when you needed her? At least they had the scrap of material.

"I told you not to move anything!" Martha exclaimed as she walked toward the back of the barn. "Why won't you listen to me?"

"Look, I only picked things up back here. I didn't touch anything else. If they want to dust for fingerprints, they have plenty of opportunities. Besides, our fingerprints are already on these things."

Mary came up behind Martha. "I've been looking over our inventory. I can't find anything missing." She frowned at Elizabeth. "What about you?"

Elizabeth shook her head. "Not a thing. I think whoever broke in was looking for something specific."

"Did either of you hear a car drive away?" Martha asked. "If our intruder was escaping, it seems we should have heard an engine…or something."

Elizabeth and Mary shook their heads.

"Nothing," Mary said. "Hey, that is odd. Obviously they parked away from the house and walked up the driveway so we wouldn't hear them." She paused for a moment. "If they planned to steal a lot, wouldn't they need a car to put it in? I mean, you can't hold as much in your hands as you can in your car."

"Not if they're only looking for one thing," Elizabeth said. "Something they could carry away without too much trouble."

"Or maybe they're Amish," Mary said. "You know, they drove their buggy."

Martha stared at her like she had cucumbers growing out of her ears. Elizabeth fought an urge to laugh. "We haven't had much trouble with Amish robbers, Mary."

"Wow, Sis," Martha said. "Do you know anything about the Amish?"

"Of course I do. I grew up here. But I know they aren't perfect."

"Of course not," Elizabeth said gently. "But I suspect we can rule out the Amish."

Mary shrugged. "Okay, fine. So you think someone parked near the road and walked to the barn?"

"Maybe," Elizabeth said. "Or they maybe were afraid we'd recognize their vehicle."

"You're right," Martha said slowly. "I hadn't thought of that."

Elizabeth headed out of the barn with the flashlight in front of her. Sure enough, the wet dirt road that led to their house showed footprints.

"Do they look like men's or women's prints?" Martha asked as she walked next to Elizabeth.

"I'm not sure," she said. "Could be a man with small feet or a woman with large feet. The only thing I can say for sure is that whoever this is was wearing sneakers. You can see the tread on the bottom. But everyone and their dog wears sneakers nowadays, so that doesn't help much."

"What about the car tracks?" Martha asked. "We could check the road…"

At that very moment, a police car turned off the main road and drove down the long dirt driveway to their house.

"Well, that's out of the question now," Elizabeth said.

The women waited as the cruiser neared them. Bird-in-Hand didn't actually have its own police department. They were covered by the East Lampeter Township Police Department.

The car pulled up next to them and two officers got out. "Got a call that you'd been robbed."

The officer who spoke had a friendly face. Elizabeth guessed him to be a few years older than she was. His dark hair was sprinkled with gray, and his steady blue eyes held a distinct hint of kindness. He was tall and had a commanding presence. Something about him encouraged trust. However, his partner, a woman probably in her late twenties, didn't look quite as accommodating.

"Yes," Elizabeth replied. "We have a secondhand shop in our barn. Someone broke in and made a mess."

"Can you tell us what's missing?" the woman asked. Her tone was no-nonsense, and suddenly Elizabeth felt a little intimidated.

Elizabeth frowned at her. "Uh, we're not sure they took anything. But they certainly caused some damage."

"They didn't steal anything?" The female officer looked annoyed.

Elizabeth felt her chest tighten. Was she making fun of them? "I'm Elizabeth Classen," she said sternly. "And these are my sisters, Martha and Mary. Who are you?"

"I'm Officer Marks," the male officer said, "and this is Officer Jackson. Why don't you show us the crime scene?"

"This way, officers," Martha said briskly.

Elizabeth could tell Martha had no intention of allowing the police to make light of their situation. Officer Marks seemed genuinely concerned, but his partner acted as if she had something more important to do. Elizabeth tried to push down her rising irritation.

The officers entered the barn, and Elizabeth showed them the broken window and the items tossed around. Then she led them to the back of the barn.

"I straightened this up some," she said, "but we left everything else alone."

"In case you want to dust for fingerprints," Martha said firmly.

Officer Jackson shook her head. "It wouldn't do any good. The public goes through here, I assume?"

Elizabeth nodded.

"Then there are too many fingerprints for us to process." She shrugged. "Besides, if nothing's been stolen—"

"Then we still need to file a report," Officer Marks said, cutting off his partner. "This is vandalism, if nothing else." He frowned at Elizabeth. "How can you be certain nothing was taken? This place is pretty full."

"I have a pretty good memory, but we'll go through our inventory list to be certain."

"That's a good idea. Let's get some information from you now, and then after you check your list you could contact me."

He smiled at Elizabeth, and she felt her heart beat a little faster. "That would be fine, Officer. What would you like us to do now?"

"Is there some place we could sit down and fill out some paperwork?"

"Would you like to come into the house? There's coffee." She pointed to a couple of chairs near the wall. "Or we could just sit over there."

"The house would be fine." He turned toward Officer Jackson. "I want you to go through everything. Make sure whoever broke in didn't leave something behind. Anything that might help us identify them. We can see the point of entry, but how did they get out? And get lots of pictures. Check around the window to see if there's any chance of fingerprints."

"But—"

"I expect a full report, Officer Jackson."

Two pink spots appeared on the young officer's cheeks. Elizabeth fought the urge to smile triumphantly at her.

"Why don't you follow me?" Martha suggested. "Maybe together we can find a clue."

Mary, who hadn't said anything to the officers, winked at Elizabeth. Strangely, Officer Jackson's attitude seemed to help the sisters shake off some of their shock over the break-in.

Elizabeth headed for the house with Officer Marks beside her. What could she share with him? Should she explain about the missing treasure? Her first instinct was to keep the real story to herself. But if Anita wasn't trying to hide the truth, why should she? Besides, the situation was beginning to get a little scary. Could they actually be in danger?

CHAPTER ELEVEN

So tell me about your shop," Officer Marks said as he sat down at the kitchen table.

After offering him a cup of coffee, which he accepted, Elizabeth briefly told him the history of Secondhand Blessings.

"So your sisters left everything to come here and run the shop with you?" he asked. "Wow. This place must mean a lot to you."

Elizabeth brought his coffee to the table. "Cream or sugar?" she asked.

He shook his head. "I like it black. Some of these flavored coffees aren't really coffee in my book."

Elizabeth laughed. "I feel the same way. Every so often, I like to indulge in a latte, but when I do, I feel like I'm having dessert, not coffee."

Officer Marks took a sip of coffee. "Mmm. This is delicious."

Elizabeth smiled at his compliment. Before she realized what she was doing, her gaze flicked to the ring finger on his left hand. No ring.

"What information do you need for your report?" She brought her mind back to the reason he was here.

Officer Marks blinked a few times and put his cup down. "Oh, sorry. I guess we should get on with it."

Elizabeth wanted to take her words back. He was being nice, and here she was rushing him, making him feel uncomfortable. He took a notepad and pen out of his pocket. "So, did you hear anything around the time of the break-in?"

Elizabeth sat down. "Yes, like a loud bang. Now that I think about it, that doesn't make sense. Wouldn't we have heard the window break when the intruder hit it?"

"Not necessarily. Breaking glass isn't that loud, especially when you're inside with the doors and windows shut."

"I wonder if it was the sound of the big table falling over," Elizabeth said.

"That's a good thought. My guess is the intruder knocked the table over on the way out. Point of entry was the window, but his exit was probably through the front entrance."

Elizabeth sighed. "Of course. I remember now that the front door wasn't locked. He must have left that way and closed the door behind him."

"You're sure you locked it earlier?"

"We must have. We're very careful about that. I should have mentioned this earlier. I'm sorry I forgot. I guess I was just shaken by what happened."

"It's understandable."

He picked up his coffee cup and drained it.

"Please, have another cup," Elizabeth said, rising from the table. She picked up the coffeepot from the counter and brought it back.

"That would be great, thanks. I have a long night ahead of me."

She poured the coffee, put the pot back, and got a loaf of pumpkin bread from the pantry. She unwrapped it, sliced it, put it on a plate, and brought it to the table, along with two plates and two forks. "Please have some of my sister Martha's pumpkin bread. It goes great with my coffee."

Although Officer Marks seemed to hesitate a moment, he finally smiled and thanked her.

Elizabeth put a slice on his plate, and one on hers, and then handed him a fork. "I put a little cinnamon in my coffee," she said. "That's why it goes so great with this bread."

His eyes widened. "That's it. Cinnamon. I've been trying to figure out what makes this taste so good. How did you ever think of that?"

Elizabeth chuckled. "I can't take credit for it. Quite a few people use cinnamon."

"Well, it's the first time I've tried it. It's amazing." He gazed around the kitchen. "This is such a cozy room. My apartment has a *modern* kitchen. It's cold and impersonal."

"Except for a new floor I put in after my mother died and a new sink, the kitchen is just as she left it. My father made this table and the cabinets."

"It's a wonderful room," he said. "I'll bet you all spend a lot of time in here."

"You'd be right. Frankly, unless we're watching television, we always gather in the kitchen. We even work on our business records here."

The policeman took a bite of the pumpkin bread and shook his head slowly. "Incredible. You should sell this."

Elizabeth smiled. "We do. Martha bakes several different things and offers them in the store."

"Well, I'm sure it sells well."

"Yes, it does. So, Officer Marks, what will happen next?"

"I'll file this report, and then we'll do whatever we can. Unfortunately, we don't have much to go on." He frowned at her. "Have there been any suspicious people in your store?"

Elizabeth almost laughed out loud. Might be easier to tell him who *wasn't* suspicious. "Actually, things have been a little weird since we opened."

"Three days? Wow. And you've already attracted this much attention? That seems a little unusual. Do you have any idea who did this? Is there some reason you're a target?"

Elizabeth made the decision to tell him the truth. At this point, a little protection from the police might not be a bad idea. She launched into the entire story. About the Smucker estate, Anita's reaction, their quest to find the articles that had been sold, and the strange woman looking for the missing painting. "Frankly, I would suspect her first. She seems to think we're hiding this picture, and she wants it. Mary told her we didn't have it, but the woman didn't seem to believe her."

"You haven't seen her yourself?"

"No. You should probably talk to Mary about her."

"Talk to me about what?"

Elizabeth hadn't heard Mary come in. She turned around to see her sister walking into the kitchen. "Officer Marks needs a description of the woman who was looking for that painting."

"Sure. What can I tell you, Officer Marks?"

"Just run through your interaction with this woman, and if you could give me a description, that would be great. Did you see her car?"

Mary recounted her contact with the woman.

"Is there anything else you can think to tell me?" he asked.

"Well, there were footprints," Elizabeth said.

"We showed them to the other officer," Mary said. "She took pictures."

"Oh!" Elizabeth said. "I almost forgot." She reached into her pocket and pulled out the small piece of fabric they'd found. "Our dog had this in his mouth. He brought it to us when we went outside. It doesn't belong to us, and we don't have any used clothing it matches."

John took the piece of cloth, put it in a baggie he had in his pocket, and stood up. "Thank you for the help," he said. "And the hospitality." He directed his last comment to Elizabeth, who smiled and nodded.

"I'll keep you up to date on our investigation." He looked at his notes and read back the telephone number Elizabeth had given him. "Is this the correct number?"

"Yes," Mary said. "There's a different number for the shop."

"I'm sorry," Elizabeth said. "I forgot to give that to you." She recited it slowly, and he wrote it down.

"I guess that's it for now," he said. "Thank you."

He walked out to the porch and joined his partner. After talking to Martha for a couple of minutes, the police officers got into their car and drove away.

CHAPTER TWELVE

Thursday, the sisters woke up to a chilly, wet day. Elizabeth sat at the kitchen table, while Mary put on a raincoat and went out to feed the animals and collect the eggs. Elizabeth's mood matched the weather. Today she planned to visit Ruth Zook, and she wasn't looking forward to it.

Martha was putting breakfast on the table when Mary came in. "Nine eggs this morning," she said with a smile. "The girls have been busy."

"With all the baking I do, I need every single egg," Martha said. She set a plate of scrambled eggs on the table and faced her sisters, her hands on her hips. "I really can't understand why our baked goods sell so well. There's a fantastic bakery in Bird-in-Hand."

"You both have specialties, Martha," Mary said. "Your banana and pumpkin breads are the best I've ever tasted."

Martha grunted. "I'll put that on my to-do list. But for now, maybe we better stick to saving our store."

Mary put the basket of eggs on the counter. After pouring herself a cup of coffee, she joined Elizabeth at the table. "Are you planning to talk to Ruth today?"

Elizabeth nodded. "I've been going over and over it in my head. Trying to figure out how to ask her about the bracelet—

and the painting. I'm not really worried about the bracelet. I mean, I can use the same line I've been giving to everyone. Put the blame on Anita. But the painting? I'll ask her if she remembers it, but what if she doesn't? At that point, there's nothing else I can do."

"You can search her house," Mary said.

Elizabeth stared at her sister in disbelief. "Sure," she said finally. "I can hear myself now. 'Excuse me, Ruth. I think you might be a thief. Do you mind if I ransack your house and search for evidence of your crime?'"

"I wouldn't put it quite that way," Martha said, sitting down next to Elizabeth. "Maybe you could be a little more diplomatic. Just ask to use the bathroom and look around on your way."

Elizabeth shook her head, taken aback that Martha would even consider such an idea. "Very funny. I have no intention of doing any such thing."

"Why not?" Mary asked. "If you can distract her—"

"Mary!" Elizabeth's emphatic rebuke caused her younger sister to jump. "I already feel terrible suspecting her in the first place."

"Being married to a pastor doesn't make you perfect," Mary said. Her pitch was a little higher than normal, a sign that she was annoyed by Elizabeth's reprimand.

"Pastor Zook and Ruth have been faithful servants for many years. There's never been a question about their honesty or sincerity. If you don't mind, I intend to believe the best about them. Frankly, I'm surprised at both of you."

Mary shrugged.

Elizabeth arched her eyebrows. "Seriously?"

"All right, all right. We should give them the benefit of the doubt."

"Thank you," Elizabeth said. She dropped the subject, but in the back of her mind she wondered if her sisters might have a point. Should she look around a bit if given the opportunity? As soon as the thought entered her mind, she pushed it away. Suspecting friends and neighbors of theft wasn't something she was comfortable with. She would be glad when this situation was settled. Hopefully, it wouldn't take long.

After praying over their food, Mary took a piece of paper out of her pocket. "I went over the riddle a little last night."

"I don't know why," Martha said. "It's unsolvable. Warren wasn't in his right mind. How could we possibly figure out what he was thinking?"

"We don't know for certain he wasn't in his right mind," Mary said, looking thoughtful. "You remember Floyd Weaver, Daddy's friend? The guy who delivered hay? He had dementia, but most days he was just fine."

"Except for the time he unloaded four bales of hay in his underwear," Martha mumbled. "Mama made us go inside the house."

Mary sighed. "But he also had times of perfect clarity. We can't automatically assume Warren wasn't cognizant when he wrote this."

"She has a point," Elizabeth said. "Things would be a lot easier if we could solve the riddle."

Mary nodded. "Yeah. It would save us time and embarrassment."

"And a lawsuit if Anita decides to go after us," Elizabeth said glumly.

"She can't sue us," Martha said, emphasizing each word. "We haven't done anything wrong. We only sold the inventory she gave us."

Elizabeth shrugged. "Maybe I'm worrying needlessly, but even if she can't hurt us legally, she could spread rumors around town that we stole something valuable from her. It could ruin our business before we even get started."

"Would people actually believe her?" Mary asked, her eyes wide.

"I have no idea, but Mama is gone. Folks in Bird-in-Hand might not trust us quite like they did when Mama was in charge."

The sisters sat quietly for a moment as Elizabeth's words sank in.

"Before we give up, let me tell you what I figured out about the riddle," Mary said.

Martha nodded at her after taking a bite of bacon. "Go for it, Sis."

"Okay, this first part? *When lightning speaks and feathers fly?* I don't think that has anything to do with pillows. When feathers fly? I think it means birds."

"I...I guess that makes sense," Elizabeth said thoughtfully. "So the first line is..."

"Thunderbird."

"But what does that mean?" Martha asked. "We weren't given anything with a thunderbird...whatever that is."

"I looked it up," Mary said. "A thunderbird is a mythical bird thought by some North American Indians to bring thunder."

"It's also a car," Martha said, her tone tinged with sarcasm, "but Anita didn't give us a car, did she? Maybe I missed it."

Mary frowned at her. "Obviously, we need to solve the rest of the riddle before it makes complete sense."

Elizabeth blew out a quick breath of air. "So we have *thunderbird* and *cousin*? What's a thunderbird's cousin?"

Mary shrugged and took another sip of coffee. "I have no idea...yet. But if we keep going, I believe it will become clear."

"I think you're delusional," Martha said, "but I know you're doing your best to help."

"Thunderbird cousin," Elizabeth said with a sigh. "Maybe Warren really was out of his head when he came up with this."

"Maybe," Mary said, "but we have to try. What else can we do?"

Elizabeth reached over and patted her sister's arm. "Thanks, Mary. Please keep working on the riddle. Of course it could help." She got up and took her dishes to the sink. "Wish I could stay with you two, but I need to get to Ruth's house. Pray for me, okay?"

"We are, Lizzie," Martha said. "If talking to Ruth doesn't yield anything, then what?"

"I think we need to concentrate on the painting and the sword." Elizabeth paused a moment, thinking. "I may run by Anita's after I see Ruth. I want to know what's going on between Uriah and the Smuckers. Why is he so upset about that sword?"

"Good idea, Sis," Mary said. She got up and carried her dishes to the counter. "Until we have an answer, we need to follow every lead."

"Which reminds me," Martha interjected. "Dorothy Mulligan called yesterday. She's bringing the frame back, but she wasn't happy about it."

"If she agreed to return it," Elizabeth said, "she must not believe the stones are real."

"I think you're right," Mary said, grinning. "If that ugly frame turns out to be Anita's treasure, I'll eat it."

"What does that frame have to do with a thunderbird or a cousin?" Martha asked sharply. "Shouldn't we start trying to match the other items Anita gave us to the riddle?"

Elizabeth slipped on the coat she'd put on the back of her chair and picked up her purse. "You're probably right, but if Warren really wasn't all there when he wrote his riddle…"

"We're wasting our time," Martha finished. She tucked a stray strand of hair behind her ear.

"Right." Elizabeth sighed deeply. "I'll get home as soon as I can. I've got my cell phone, so call me if anything important happens."

"We'll be fine," Mary said. "We can get along without you, you know."

Elizabeth patted her sister on the arm. "I know that, but I like to think you need me."

Mary caught her by the hand. "All the time, Lizzie," she said softly. "All the time."

As Elizabeth drove away from the house, the rain began to come down harder, echoing her own stormy emotions.

CHAPTER THIRTEEN

As Mary and Martha slogged through the mud to the barn, Mary wondered if people would stay away because of the weather. However, minutes after they opened, several cars pulled in and parked next to the barn. Frankly, the idea of a slow day sounded wonderful. Even though they'd only been open three days, she was tired. A lot of it was probably stress caused by the situation with Anita Smucker.

Mary was determined to solve the riddle and get Anita off their backs, but so far the clues hadn't made much sense. As she rolled the words over in her head, the door opened, and Dorothy Mulligan stepped into the barn. Dorothy's hair was dyed a bright fuchsia color, and when she spoke she reminded Mary of a chirping bird.

"What can I do for you, Dorothy?" Mary asked, smiling.

"You can give me back every penny I spent on this cheap frame." She thrust a plastic grocery bag at Mary. "I paid ten dollars."

Mary took the package. "You must have this confused with another item. I believe this frame was marked five dollars."

Dorothy's eyes narrowed to small slits. "You don't know what you're talking about. I want my ten dollars. Now."

A couple of other customers turned to watch the tantrum Dorothy seemed determined to pitch.

"I'm sorry, Dorothy," Mary choked out. "I must have confused your purchase with someone else's. If you'll follow me to the register, I'll be happy to give you a full refund."

It took every ounce of will Mary had not to lash out at the woman, but Lizzie had drilled into Mary and Martha that, unless it was something outrageous, the "customer is always right."

"Can you give Dorothy back the ten dollars she spent on this frame?" Mary asked Martha as they approached the register. Martha started to say something, but Mary shook her head slightly, trying to stay out of Dorothy's line of sight. Martha frowned but kept her mouth shut as she handed Dorothy a ten-dollar bill.

Dorothy grabbed the money and left without another word.

"What was that about?" Martha asked.

"She insisted she paid ten dollars."

"It was five."

Mary sighed. "I know that, Sis. But she was getting ready to pitch a fit, and I remembered what Lizzie said."

"That the customer is always right?"

"Yeah."

Martha shook her head. "But at the same time, we shouldn't let people like Dorothy Mulligan rob us."

"It's five dollars. I'd gladly pay it just to get rid of her."

"I see your point." Martha held out her hand. "Let's see the frame. I still say the stones are cheap colored glass."

Mary opened the plastic grocery bag and pulled the frame out. "Oh my goodness!" she exclaimed loudly.

"What's wrong?"

Mary turned the frame around to show Martha. Several of the stones were missing.

Martha stood up and walked over to peer closely at the old frame. "She removed some of the stones."

"Including the large one." Mary studied the frame. "Interesting. Maybe this is what we've been looking for."

"Maybe," Martha said slowly. She gently pried one of the smaller green stones off the frame and held it up to the light. "This certainly isn't real," she said. "Look at it."

Mary leaned in and stared at the stone Martha held. It was cloudy and full of discolorations. Obviously not a real gemstone. "So why would Dorothy remove the other fake jewels? It doesn't make sense."

Martha put the shiny green stone down on the counter. "No, it doesn't, does it? Let's give her a call and ask her."

Mary looked at her sister in horror. "I'm not calling her. You saw how nasty she was."

Martha snorted. "Who cares what she thinks? I don't. I just want the truth."

"Then you call her."

Martha put the frame down and picked up a Bird-in-Hand telephone directory. She stored the number into her cell phone, and after helping a few customers over the next half hour, she had time to give Dorothy a call.

"Dorothy, this is Martha Classen Watts. Sorry to bother you, but I need to ask you a question about the frame you returned to us today."

She was quiet as she listened to Dorothy's response. Martha rolled her eyes and put her free hand over her mouth as if trying to hold back laughter. "Yes, I'm sure this has been very traumatic for you," she said through her fingers. "I'm so sorry about that."

Another pause. Mary wanted to know what Dorothy was saying—and yet she didn't. "I understand," Martha was saying. "Is this how you discovered the frame wasn't quite what you'd hoped?"

Mary waited while Martha listened, but she could feel her blood begin to boil. Wasn't what she'd hoped? What did that mean?

Finally, Martha said goodbye and hung up.

"So what did she say?" Mary asked.

"She said she planned to return it anyway because the stones were falling out. She accused us of cheating her."

"We cheated her? Oh brother." Mary rolled her eyes.

Martha sighed. "Well, I think we can rule the frame out. There's no way this cheap frame ever had valuable gemstones."

"Unless someone purposely tried to hide them in the frame, thinking everyone would assume all the stones were glass."

Martha shook her head. "Sorry, but I truly don't think Dorothy is smart enough to tell the difference between valuable gemstones and cheap glass. I think the stones really did fall out."

Mary raised an eyebrow. "This frame *is* pretty old, right? What are the chances that the stones would just suddenly start falling out?"

Martha stared at her sister. "You're right. That doesn't make sense. Unless the frame isn't old, and the picture was recently added to it."

"But why would anyone do that? A picture that no one cared about stuck in a new frame? And why pick an ugly frame like this?"

Martha grinned. "One man's treasure…"

"Maybe so," Mary admitted. "But the Smuckers always seemed to have good taste. This frame doesn't seem to fit their style."

"I think I might know the answer."

Mary looked at her sister questioningly.

"Do you remember that terrible purse Jennifer bought for you once? The one with a sparkly peacock on the front?"

Mary laughed. "She got it at a yard sale and thought it was the most beautiful purse in the world. I carried it whenever I went anywhere with her. It was pretty embarrassing." She paused a moment. "Oh, I see what you're trying to say. This could have been a gift. Maybe Anita's parents couldn't bear to get rid of it because Anita gave it to them."

"Exactly."

Mary nodded. "Good thought, Sis. I wonder if we could ask Anita about it?"

The women mulled the idea over for a moment.

"I think I'll call her," Martha said.

"All right," Mary said slowly. "If you think it's okay."

"Why are you afraid of upsetting her? Maybe she needs to worry about irritating us."

Mary smiled at Martha. "Okay, call. If we can rule the frame out, it will be one less thing to worry about."

Martha had just picked up her phone when a woman approached them, asking about cookware. Mary took her over to the area with pots, pans, and baking dishes. After haggling on the prices a bit, the woman picked two frying pans, a metal saucepan, and a large stewpot. Mary helped her carry the items to the front of the store. Martha was already off the phone and quickly checked the woman out. Once she was out of earshot, Martha nodded at Mary.

"You were right. The frame was a gift to Anita's father when Anita was a child."

"Odd that she didn't want to keep it."

Martha shrugged. "Probably can't keep everything. Funny thing is, when I told her some of the stones were missing, she seemed a little upset."

"The frame may have meant more to her than she realized."

"I think that's it."

"Well, at least we can rule it out. That's one item off our list."

Martha sighed. "Little by little, bit by bit, I guess."

Mary chuckled. "Mama used to say that all the time."

"She was right. It's all we can do."

Mary shrugged and went to help a man looking at fishing equipment. Would they ever find Anita's treasure? She was beginning to wonder. Hopefully Lizzie was making progress.

CHAPTER FOURTEEN

After calling Ruth to make certain it was all right for her to stop by, Elizabeth continued to play over and over in her mind what she would say when she faced her pastor's wife. So far, nothing she came up with felt right. She could certainly explain the bracelet—but what could she say about the painting? Once she asked whether Ruth had seen it, if she denied it, Elizabeth had nowhere else to go. She couldn't push the point without making it sound as if she didn't believe her.

Should she tell Ruth they were looking for something very valuable? Or would that actually make it worse? As if she suspected Ruth might have sold the bracelet or the painting because she wanted the money?

She pulled into the driveway of the Zooks' modest home, full of dread. As if berating her for her mistrust, the rain increased, hitting the roof of Elizabeth's car, creating a loud din that certainly didn't calm her nerves.

She grabbed her umbrella, got out, and hurried to the front door, where Ruth was already waiting for her.

"Oh, honey," Ruth said with a smile. "Your shoes are wet. I'm sure your feet are cold. You get in here, and I'll get you warmed up."

Elizabeth stepped inside, feeling guilty. Ruth's kind concern only made everything worse.

"Let me have that coat," she said, holding out her hand. "You go into the kitchen. I've got hot coffee and warm coffee cake right from the oven."

Elizabeth let Ruth help pull off her drenched coat. "Thank you, Ruth," she said. "It wasn't raining much earlier, but it seems to be getting worse. It's turning into quite a downpour."

Realizing she was blathering because of her nerves, Elizabeth forced her mouth shut, determined to get through this situation without making a fool of herself. After Ruth hung Elizabeth's coat on the coatrack, she followed the older woman into her warm kitchen. Although the furniture and appliances weren't expensive, Ruth had created a warm, inviting kitchen with a lot of personal touches. Actually, it reminded Elizabeth of their own kitchen, but Ruth's had a collection of roosters ranging from full-sized ceramic centerpieces to salt and pepper shakers and every imaginable collectible in between

"Would you rather sit in the living room?" Ruth asked. She smiled at Elizabeth. "I know you and your sisters spend a lot of time in your kitchen, like I do, but we don't have to stay in here."

"It's fine," Elizabeth said. "Feels more like home." She sat down at the kitchen table. Elizabeth loved the red Formica top and matching red chairs. Actually, the chairs were quite comfortable.

"Just a minute," Ruth said. She left the room and came back shortly with a pair of fluffy slippers. "You put these on, hon. They're brand new, never been worn. Harold gave them to me for my birthday, but I wanted to wear out my other pair before starting on a new one."

"Oh, Ruth. I can't wear your new slippers."

"Don't be silly. Your feet must be frozen. Put these on. I don't want to hear another word about it."

Elizabeth shook off her wet loafers and slid her feet into the fluffy slippers. She had to admit they felt great.

"Now, isn't that better?" Ruth went to the counter, poured a cup of coffee, and brought it to Elizabeth. "And let me get you a piece of this good coffee cake."

Elizabeth sat there with a smile pasted on her face. She was feeling less and less motivated to ask Ruth the questions she'd come here to pose. Frankly, she was about ready to forget her entire reason for visiting, but there really wasn't any way she could do that. Eventually she'd have to confront Ruth. She nervously cleared her throat. "I—I heard you and Pastor Zook are finally going to retire."

Ruth stopped cutting the cake and turned around, a wide smile on her face. "Yes. You heard right." A wrinkle of concern creased her forehead, but before Elizabeth could respond, Ruth hastened to say, "Please understand that we love the church. We're not retiring because we're unhappy. We just… Well, we're just ready for a rest. Our son in Florida bought us a small house. With our social security we believe we can just make ends meet. We love the ocean, and we love our son and his family. We couldn't ask for anything more."

"That sounds wonderful, Ruth. I'm so glad." And she really was. Especially since she felt rather certain now that Ruth hadn't sold Anita's treasure. Relief washed through her.

Ruth plopped a big piece of coffee cake onto a small plate, got a fork, and carried it over to the table. She handed it to Elizabeth and sat down across from her.

"Enough about us. You wanted to see me about something?"

Elizabeth nodded. "Anita Smucker contacted us on Monday. She consigned to us quite a few items from her home—many of them belonging to her parents—and she asked us to sell them in the shop. Now she wants them all back." Elizabeth put a piece of coffee cake in her mouth. It was delicious. Cinnamon, pecans, and butter exploded on her tongue. "This is incredible," she said to Ruth. "You're such an excellent baker."

"Thank you," Ruth said. "I'm so glad you like it." Her smile slipped a little. "So she wants the bracelet back? I bought it for Susan's birthday."

Susan was the Zooks' daughter who lived in Wyoming. "Have you already mailed it?" Elizabeth asked.

Ruth nodded. "It went out yesterday."

Elizabeth sighed. "I understand."

"I hate to disappoint Anita. Is there a reason she's asking for everything to be returned?"

Elizabeth picked up her coffee cup and took a long, slow sip. The story was that Anita had decided she wasn't ready to sell her parents' things, but Elizabeth was sure she could trust her friend with the entire truth. "Look, I want to tell you something, but I need to ask you to keep it to yourself."

"Is it because she may have accidentally given you something very valuable?"

Elizabeth gulped with surprise. "Where did you hear that?"

Ruth's brown eyes sparkled. "It was a major topic of conversation at the Two Bird Café the last time I was there. I'm not sure who started the rumor, but I suspect it was Anita's hairdresser.

She's kind of a blabbermouth." Ruth's face flushed. "I don't mean to be judgmental. But… Well, you know…"

In spite of being upset to learn that the truth was out, Elizabeth couldn't hold back a smile. "Yes, I know. Peggy's a fine person, but she does love to gossip."

"Yes, that she does." She took a sip of coffee and then set the cup down, a frown deepening the lines on her forehead. "You think the bracelet might be this piece she's looking for?"

"I have no idea. We're looking at every possibility. Anita insists we locate everything she gave us. I had to ask Esther Vogel to give back two skillets and some pillowcases. It was really embarrassing."

"I'm sure Esther was very gracious."

"Yes, she was. I've got some replacements in my car for her. I think she'll be even happier with them." Elizabeth picked up her purse and pulled out a long box. "This bracelet belonged to my mother. It's not an heirloom or anything, so please don't worry about that. Daddy got it for her when they were younger, before we were born, but she never really wore it. Just wasn't her style. But it's beautiful, and I believe Susan would love it. I would really like to give it to you so you can replace the other bracelet—if Susan agrees to return it. If not, it's fine with us."

"Oh, honey, I can't take your bracelet."

"Don't be silly. We want you to have it."

Frowning, Ruth opened the box and gasped when she saw the bracelet. It was made of diamond-like rhinestones, accented by a thin line of blue stones running through the middle. "Why, it's lovely. Why wouldn't your mother wear it?"

"She put it on a few times when she and my father went out somewhere or when the church had what she called a 'dress-up' party. You knew my mom. Jeans and a sweatshirt almost every day. A hard worker who didn't take much to dresses. When she left the ultraconservative ways of her parents' Mennonite tradition, the last thing she wanted to wear was a dress, other than to church, that is."

Ruth chuckled and self-consciously smoothed her dark blue skirt. "I understand how she feels. I bought some jeans, some slacks, and even a couple of pairs of shorts for Florida. Not short shorts, of course. But they're still shorts."

Elizabeth smiled at Ruth's thinking she had to qualify her choice of shorts. She was pretty sure the seventy-three-year-old woman wouldn't be hitting the beach in short shorts. That would definitely give the people in Bird-in-Hand something to gossip about. "You and Pastor Zook are going to have a great time in Florida. Maybe we'll come and visit you sometime."

"Oh, honey, we'd love that."

As Elizabeth got ready to take another bite of coffee cake, she remembered the painting. She put her fork down. "Ruth, do you recall seeing a painting among the items Anita gave us? It would have been in the inventory room at the back of the barn. We have no idea where it went and can't figure out what happened to it. Do you remember it?"

"Why, yes, I do," she said. "I most certainly do remember. It was a young girl with a cat in her lap, right?"

"Yes, that's it." Elizabeth was shocked that Ruth recalled the painting. "It never made it to the shop. Do you have any idea why?"

Ruth stared at her for a moment, her eyebrows knit together and her eyes narrowed. "It was removed not long after Anita's belongings were first delivered. One afternoon while I was helping out and working alone."

"Removed? Removed by whom?"

"Why, I thought you knew. It was Anita."

CHAPTER FIFTEEN

It was a little after one o'clock when Elizabeth rang Anita's doorbell. After learning from Ruth that Anita had reclaimed the painting, Elizabeth was determined to find out just what was going on.

As she waited for someone to answer the door, Elizabeth looked over the large yard. The gardens that Warren Smucker had prided himself on were in need of care. Although it was just early spring, weeds were beginning to grow in the flower beds, something Warren would never have allowed. And the bushes were looking ragged from lack of trimming.

Although the house itself appeared to be in good shape, Elizabeth had to wonder if it would also fall into disrepair. Unless Anita could find what her father had left for her, she might actually be forced to sell it. The large brick two-story with its huge white pillars should be worth quite a bit, but obviously the home meant a lot to Anita. Elizabeth understood why she didn't want to leave. She felt the same way about the house and land that had been in her own family for so long.

Elizabeth had just raised her hand to punch the bell one more time when the door suddenly swung open. Anita stood on the other side, glowering at her.

"I hope you've brought me more of my things," she said, her small face tight and her thin lips pursed.

"No, but I've come to talk to you about a couple of them. May I come in?"

Although she didn't look excited to welcome Elizabeth into her home, Anita slowly pulled the door open.

The last time Elizabeth had been inside the Smucker place was almost two years ago when she'd attended the yearly Christmas party Warren used to throw. Last year, his health was such that he wasn't able to arrange the party. Several people, including Elizabeth, wondered why Anita hadn't taken over the tradition. Now Elizabeth wondered if it was because there wasn't enough money.

The inside of the house still spoke of comfort and good taste. Although Elizabeth could clearly see that there were fewer decorations, it didn't look sparse. Though some people in town thought Warren had gone overboard with collecting and displaying his treasures, it wasn't because he was proud. He truly loved unique antiques and collectibles and thought other people would appreciate them too. In fact, he was known to give away possessions when someone complimented him on a particular item. Elizabeth's mother had a lovely vase that Warren had given her when she admired it. She'd kept it in the china closet and had used it every spring when her purple irises bloomed.

"Please, have a seat," Anita said, her voice nasal and her words clipped.

Elizabeth thanked her and sat down.

"Coffee?"

Elizabeth shook her head. "No, but thank you." Actually, she would love a cup of hot coffee, but she was fairly certain Anita was just being polite and didn't really want her to stay that long.

"Can I ask what items you've collected so far?"

Elizabeth quickly mentioned what things she could remember, including the skillets and pillowcases she took from Esther Vogel. To her credit, Anita looked a little embarrassed about Esther.

"Is that it?" she asked when Elizabeth stopped talking and looked down at her hands.

"Ruth Zook sent the bracelet she bought to her daughter. I would really rather she not have to ask for it to be mailed back, but if you insist on doing so, you can ask her."

Anita shook her head. "The bracelet is costume jewelry, I'm certain of it. I don't need it back."

"There was one other thing I had to ask Ruth about," Elizabeth said, frowning. "A painting. It disappeared from our inventory—before we even had a chance to display it."

Anita shifted positions on the couch and looked away. She clasped her hands together so tightly, her knuckles turned white.

"I assume you know what she told me."

"That I took the painting back."

"Yes." Elizabeth cleared her throat. "Mary looked up that painting on the internet. She found out the original was stolen, and that it was worth a great deal of money. I have to ask you—"

Before she could finish her sentence, Anita laughed.

This certainly wasn't the reaction Elizabeth had been expecting.

"No, it isn't an original Torelli," Anita said. "My father painted it. It's a copy. I didn't realize it until I found a note about it in his papers. It hung in the bedroom, and I assumed it was real. When I began to do research, trying to find out the value of everything, I found out about the Torelli. Of course, I was horrified. How could my father have a stolen painting in his possession? That's when I went back and took the painting. I found out the truth after that. To say I was relieved is an understatement." She sighed and shook her head. "Although I can't say that I wouldn't be happy to get the amount the original is worth. To be honest, he did such a great job of replicating it, I'm afraid others will think it is an authentic Torelli as well. Selling it could cause more trouble than either one of us wants to deal with. Besides, I think I know what I want to do with it. Something my father would approve of."

"My sisters and I will keep looking," Elizabeth said, "but please don't remove anything else without telling us. It's very confusing."

"I won't. At this point, I'm just grasping at straws anyway. I haven't found anything that's really valuable. And the riddle is still a riddle." She actually smiled at Elizabeth. "Are you sure you don't want a cup of coffee?"

Relieved by Anita's change in attitude, Elizabeth returned the smile. "You know, that would be nice. Thank you."

When Anita got up to go to the kitchen, Elizabeth slid her jacket off and made herself more comfortable. At least the mystery of the painting was solved, and the bracelet wouldn't have to be returned. Two good results so far. Now she planned to ask about the sword. She was a little worried about broaching the subject. Warren Smucker had been a kind man who'd made a lot of friends, but there were stories about his reaction when he felt betrayed. A shrewd businessman, he'd also been known to have a much harsher side when the need arose. Elizabeth saw seeds of Warren's disposition in his daughter. Elizabeth wasn't sure from one moment to the next how Anita would act in certain situations. Now that Anita was calmer, Elizabeth didn't want to stir the waters again.

A few minutes later, Anita came back carrying a tray with coffee cups and a beautiful silver pot. "I forgot to ask you how you take your coffee, so I brought sugar, sweetener, and cream."

"Oh, Anita. You didn't have to go to all that trouble. I usually drink it black."

Anita shook her head as she put the tray on the carved mahogany coffee table. "Not a problem, but you should try this cream. It's heavenly."

"Thank you." Elizabeth sometimes took cream in her coffee, but for the most part she turned it down so she could avoid the calories.

Anita poured two cups of coffee and put a little cream in both cups. Then she handed one of them to Elizabeth. She sat down again, and the women sipped their coffee. The silence began to make Elizabeth feel a little nervous. Finally, she decided to raise the subject of the sword before she chickened out.

"I do have a question, Anita," she said carefully. "It has to do with Uriah Barnhart."

Anita's expression went flat, making Elizabeth hesitant to proceed.

"What does Mr. Barnhart have to do with anything?" As soon as the words left Anita's mouth, a look of horror replaced her previous pensive expression. "Please don't tell me you sold him my father's sword."

Elizabeth, confused by her statement, nodded slowly. "As a matter of fact, we did. If you didn't want it sold, why would you even give it to us?"

Anita stood up, almost spilling her coffee. "I never thought Uriah would buy it. I thought he'd left town long ago."

"He was gone for a while, but he recently moved back."

Anita swatted at the air as if Elizabeth's comment was an annoying insect. Then she sat down and put her coffee cup on the table. She pointed at Elizabeth, her face rigid with anger. "You've got to get it back. My father would roll over in his grave if he knew Uriah had that sword."

"I don't understand. Why shouldn't Uriah have the sword?"

Anita folded her hands together as if she were getting ready to pray. "He shouldn't have the sword, Elizabeth, because it was used to murder my great-great-grandfather!"

CHAPTER SIXTEEN

For a moment, Elizabeth was too shocked to speak. She simply stared at Anita. "What on earth do you mean?" she asked finally.

Anita reached up and patted her perfectly coiffed hair as if making certain it was still holding its shape. It was something she did quite often. Elizabeth wondered if it was a nervous habit, or if she really was worried about how she looked.

"Our great-great-grandfathers were friends," she said. "Good friends. They joined the Union army together and fought side by side. But something happened. Some kind of disagreement. My great-great-grandfather, Gideon Smucker, was killed, and Uriah's relative took his sword. My father fought for years to get it back. Even through legal means, but he could never prove the sword originally belonged to Gideon Smucker."

"But somehow he ended up with it," Elizabeth said. "I mean, you had it."

"Yes, I did. And I should have kept it. When I was deciding what to keep and what to sell, for some reason I felt the need to get rid of it. It's a symbol of something…awful. But now it seems I've made another mistake. Uriah has the sword, but he can't be allowed to keep it. I *must* have it back." She leaned over a bit, drawing closer to Elizabeth. "I will pay you a thousand dollars to bring me that sword. It's very important."

"I can't do that. This seems to be something personal between you and Uriah. We sold the sword in good faith. You never told us not to sell it to Uriah Barnhart."

Anita rose and stood over Elizabeth. "You continue to block me no matter what I say or do. I want my possessions back, and I want them back immediately, do you hear me?"

Her voice had taken on a hysterical tone, and Elizabeth felt it was best to leave before things got out of control. She put her coffee cup down, pulled on her jacket, and stood up. "We're doing all we can to get your things back, Anita, but we're doing it as a favor to you. Not because we have to. Your threats to sue us are baseless. We both know that. However, if you can't be civil, we'll have to stop and let you take care of this yourself. You caused this situation, not us."

With that, she picked up her purse and headed for the front door. Thankfully, Anita didn't call her back. She was trembling as she got into the car, but it had nothing to do with the temperature outside. Maybe they should have refused to help Anita from the outset. Trying to be accommodating was backfiring badly. Was Anita bad-mouthing them all over town? Would it hurt their business? Elizabeth couldn't be sure. As she drove back to the farm, all she could do was pray her words hadn't just destroyed Secondhand Blessings before they really got started.

Martha couldn't help worrying about Elizabeth. How was her meeting with Ruth going? She'd been gone a long time. Shouldn't she be back by now?

Mary came walking up to the counter. "I need something from the house. Want anything while I'm in there?"

"I'd love a glass of lemonade," she said. "And maybe a couple of those peanut butter cookies I made yesterday?"

Mary smiled. "You've got it. Think I'll get some for myself as well." She patted her flat stomach. "Your cooking is dangerous. I'm going to have to watch it unless I want to buy bigger clothes."

Martha snorted. "With that metabolism of yours? Impossible. You've always eaten whatever you wanted and never gained an ounce. It seems I can't get rid of these extra fifteen pounds. And I've had them ever since Craig was born over three decades ago!"

Mary laughed. "Things change when we get older."

"Don't I know it," Martha said with a sigh. "I can't eat half of what I used to. It's very discouraging."

Mary laughed. "You'll be fine. You look great."

"Right after Chuck died, I gained almost thirty pounds. I finally got it off, but it was really hard. I guess I'll have to learn to live proudly with my extra 'Craig pounds.'"

Mary reached for her sister's hand. "I'm sorry for everything you've been through, Martha. I really am."

"I know you are, sweetie. Thanks."

Martha watched as her sister headed to the house. Mary could drive Martha up the wall sometimes with her scatterbrained ways, but she'd always been compassionate. Her sweet nature was something Martha wished she had more of. She knew she tended to see things in black and white—without much gray. Maybe Mary's caring disposition would rub off on her a little.

Mary had just gone inside the house when a woman entered the store. She nodded at Martha and headed toward the back of the barn as if she knew exactly what she was looking for. Pal, who'd been lying next to Martha's feet, stirred and began to emit a low growl. Martha stared down at him. What was that about? Feeling a little alarmed, she stood up and began to follow the woman, with Pal on her heels, still rumbling his displeasure.

"Is there something I can help you with?" she asked the woman, who had stopped at the display of pictures and paintings at the back of the barn.

She shook her head. "No. I'm just looking for something specific. You don't seem to have it." She stared down at Pal, whose throaty grumble was a little unnerving.

The woman scanned the pictures on the wall once again. "When will you get in new paintings?"

"There's no certain time. We just put them up when they come in." Martha frowned at the woman. "Can you tell me just what you're looking for?"

Before the woman could answer, a voice came from behind them. "She's looking for a copy of the Torelli painting, aren't you?"

Martha turned around to find Mary scowling at them. "This is the woman who was here the other day, and I just remembered where I saw that piece of fabric we found after the break-in. It's from the blouse you were wearing the last time you were here." She glanced down at her feet. "Sneakers. Just like the tracks in the mud outside."

The woman's face fell. "I...Yes, it was me. I'm sorry I was so rude to you the other day. It's...it's not like me."

"But it's like you to break into our barn?" Martha asked.

The woman stared at them wide-eyed until she finally broke down and began to cry. "I—I'm sorry. You see, my daughter loves that painting. I've tried to buy a copy of it, but even the copies are terribly expensive, and we just can't afford it. Not with all the hospital bills."

"I don't understand," Martha said.

The woman sighed and pushed a lock of hair from her face. Martha noticed the tiredness in her eyes and the dark circles beneath them.

"My daughter, Kelly, has cancer. Leukemia. Everything we have is going toward the medicine and the hospital costs."

"What made you think we had the painting?" Mary asked. "Even we didn't know it at first."

"I—I used to work for the Smuckers," the woman said, "as a maid. I'd seen the painting at their house. When Mr. Smucker died, his daughter let me go. Mr. Smucker knew Kelly loved the painting, and before he passed away he told me he was going to leave it for her. Before I left, I asked Anita about it, and she told me the painting was being sold. That she needed the money." She hung her head. "She said she'd given it to you. That's why I came here. To buy it. When you told me you didn't have it, I didn't believe you. I was so desperate I came back and broke in. I thought maybe I could find it." She shook her head. "I'm so ashamed. I've never done anything like that before in my life. I just wanted something to make Kelly smile again. It's all I could think to do. I guess I went a little crazy. I'm so terribly sorry. Can you ever forgive me?" She looked at the boarded-up window on the side of the barn. "Of course I'll pay for a new window and anything I broke. I didn't mean for that to happen."

Before Martha could respond, Mary wrapped her arms around the woman. "Don't worry about it. And yes, we forgive you. We'll also try to find that painting. If it's in our power, we'll make sure your daughter gets it."

Martha frowned at her sister. How could she possibly promise something like that?

The woman sobbed as Mary held her. When Mary released her, she wiped the tears from her eyes with the back of her hand. "I'm Eleanor Wallace."

"Mary Baxter," Mary said. "And this is my sister Martha Watts."

Eleanor held her hand out, and Mary shook it. Then she extended her hand to Martha, who also took it. She'd just let go when she noticed Elizabeth standing a few feet away, listening.

"Didn't know you were back," Martha said. "We've been wondering about you."

"Elizabeth, this is Eleanor Wallace. She used to..."

"Work for the Smuckers," Elizabeth finished. "I heard."

"Did you find out anything about the painting?" Mary asked.

Elizabeth flushed and looked away for a moment. "We need to talk," she said. Then she smiled at Eleanor. "Could you give my sister your phone number?" she asked. "We'll call you as soon as we have something to tell you."

Eleanor nodded. "Of course. I'd be happy to. And...thanks for not having me arrested. I really am terribly ashamed of my actions. All I can say is that I'm not myself right now."

Mary put her hand on Eleanor's back and began guiding her toward the front counter. "Come with me, and I'll get your contact information."

As they walked away, Martha noticed Elizabeth's worried expression. "Is something wrong?" she asked.

"I'm not sure," she said. "But I may have just ruined Eleanor's chances of getting that painting for her daughter."

CHAPTER SEVENTEEN

That evening, the sisters gathered around the kitchen table once again. Although the rain had stopped and it had turned into a beautiful spring day, once the sun had gone down, the temp had gone down with it, and Martha's homemade stew helped warm Elizabeth from the inside out. While Elizabeth shared the details of her visit with Ruth and Anita, Martha and Mary ate. Every few minutes, she'd stop and take a bite. In truth, she wanted nothing more than to concentrate on her supper and forget the events of the day. When she dipped her spoon into the stew once again, Mary spoke up.

"At least you know Ruth isn't a crook," she said with a smile.

After swallowing, Elizabeth pointed her spoon at her sister. "I never thought she was a crook. I just…" She sighed and put the spoon back in her bowl. "Maybe I did. I don't know anymore. Right now, everyone seems suspicious."

"So Anita was okay until you brought up the sword?" Martha asked. "But why would she get upset with you? You had nothing to do with it."

Elizabeth shrugged. "She just wants it back. She thought Uriah had left town. It had never entered her mind that he would end up buying the sword. She even offered me one thousand dollars to bring it to her."

Mary gasped. "Really? Is it in his house?"

"Mary!" Martha said. "Don't even think about it. We're not going to steal that sword. Not for any amount of money."

"I know," Mary said, her bottom lip jutting out in a slight pout. "It was just a thought."

"Well, it was a bad thought," Elizabeth said. "Now we need to figure out how to make Anita happy, so she'll give that painting to Kelly."

Martha sighed loudly. "Sometimes I wonder if we'll still be looking for Anita's so-called treasure ten years from now. Has it occurred to you that it might not even be among the items she gave us? What if it's something still in the house?"

"Anita hired an appraiser after she found her father's letter. He couldn't find anything in the house with as much value as the letter indicated. That's when she decided she must have given it to us."

"But we still don't know for certain."

Elizabeth nodded. "You're right. What if Warren imagined the whole thing? And here we're running around like crazy people, trying to find something that doesn't exist."

"I, for one, think it exists," Mary said.

Martha sighed and leaned back in her chair, folding her arms across her chest. "And just how did you come up with that?" she asked. "Do you have some kind of special insight the rest of us don't?"

Mary frowned at her. "No. It's just that… Well, it's the riddle. It just seems…specific. Like it was written by someone who knew exactly what he was talking about."

Martha shook her head slowly. "I don't know…"

"Actually, I agree," Elizabeth said. "It feels like something…real."

"But we have to accept the possibility that Warren was confused when he wrote it," Martha said.

Mary got up and went over to the kitchen drawer where they kept the riddle. "Let's try again," she said. "Maybe this time something will pop out at us that we missed before."

The last thing Elizabeth wanted to do was listen to that silly riddle again, but she knew if they could solve it, the situation with Anita might very well come to an end. And she was willing to do anything to make that happen.

Mary brought the paper over to the table. "Okay, here we go.

'*When lightning speaks and feathers fly,*
And your mother's sister's child makes dirty pies,
You'll find yourself feeling quite continental.
Open your eyes, and you'll see the truth.
Hidden in shadows and very sentimental.'"

"So far we've decided that when lightning speaks and feathers fly translates into *thunderbird*," Martha said. "And your mother's sister's child is your *cousin*."

"What in the world do thunderbirds and cousins have to do with anything?" Elizabeth asked, unable to keep her frustration in check. "Doesn't make sense."

"Wait a minute," Mary said. "'*You'll find yourself feeling quite continental.* A Thunderbird is a car. So is a Continental."

"We've been through this already," Martha snapped. "We don't have any cars. And besides, what do cars have to do with someone's cousin?" She grabbed her bowl, pushed her chair back, and got up. "I don't want to hear this stupid riddle anymore. I wake up in the middle of the night trying to solve it. I think Warren was out of his mind, and this riddle is proof of it."

"Is there anything Anita gave us that connects to this riddle in any way?" Elizabeth asked, trying to calm her sister. "That's the question we should be asking ourselves."

"Well, let's see," Martha said, her tone sarcastic. "We don't have any cars. And we don't know Anita's cousins. So...no. Nothing she gave us lines up with this stupid riddle. Nothing."

"Wait a minute," Elizabeth said slowly. "Didn't you tell me you took pictures of some of Anita's things when they came in, Mary?"

"Yeah. To help Martha set up the inventory book."

"What about the sword?"

"I...I think so. I'm pretty sure I did."

"Can I see it?"

Mary got up and left the room. When she came back she had her phone in her hand. "Hopefully, I didn't erase it. I meant to delete all the pictures once Martha was finished, but you know me. Sometimes I get behind."

For once, Elizabeth was grateful Mary was scatterbrained. She might be wrong, but she had an idea that might actually help them. "Can you pull up a picture of the sword?"

Mary scrolled through her pictures for a couple of minutes. Then she stopped. "Here it is. I have a couple of shots, but unfortunately, they're not very clear."

She handed her phone to Elizabeth, and Elizabeth nodded when she looked at it. "Look at the scabbard. Would you call that a thunderbird?"

She passed it to Martha, who stared at it for a moment. "I don't know," she said slowly. "This picture is so fuzzy. I mean, it kind of looks like an eagle. What does a thunderbird look like?"

"I don't know, but look at what he's holding in his talons."

Martha peered closer. "Could it be bolts of lightning?"

Elizabeth nodded. "Look, even if this is an eagle, it's still a 'thunderbird,' right? I mean, it's a bird with thunderbolts in its talons. Get it?"

Martha handed the phone back to Mary. "Maybe. Frankly, I'd need to see better pictures. Or better yet, the sword itself before I could really tell you if this fits the riddle. But even if you're right, what does that have to do with a cousin?"

Elizabeth snorted. "I have no idea. Maybe the sword got back to the Smuckers through one of their cousins. Anita didn't say anything about that. But I believe the riddle is pointing to the sword. It has to be. This is the only thing that makes sense."

"You might be right," Martha said, "but in my research, I couldn't find anything that would make me think it was worth very much."

"Must be something about this particular sword we don't know," Mary said. "Maybe the rest of the riddle will make it clearer." She stared at the paper in front of her. "The sword originally belonged to the Smuckers, so I guess that makes it sentimental."

"Sentimental?" Elizabeth said sharply. "Gideon Smucker was killed with it! How could that be sentimental?"

Mary and Martha just stared at Elizabeth. She knew she sounded a little manic, but the riddle, dealing with Anita...all of it was getting to be too much.

Martha started to say something when the house's landline rang. Mary jumped up and grabbed the phone. After she said hello, she asked the caller to hold on a moment. Then she handed the phone to Elizabeth.

"It's a man," she whispered. "I don't recognize the voice."

"Hello?" Elizabeth said, hoping this wasn't more bad news.

"Miss Classen? This is John. John Marks. The police officer. Remember me? I do hope I'm not bothering you."

Elizabeth felt her face grow hot. She got up from her chair and carried the phone into the living room. "No, we just finished supper," she said. "I'm not busy."

"Good." John cleared his throat. "Say, I know this is kind of out of the blue, you might say, but there's a play at the Bird-in-Hand Stage Saturday night. I hear it's good. I wondered if you'd like to go to the show and then out to dinner?"

Although Elizabeth tried to find a way to explain that her life was too busy to take time off at the moment, out of her mouth came the words, "Why, yes. I'd love to." She almost put her hand over her mouth in shock. Why had she said that?

"Wonderful," John said. "The play starts at six. I'll pick you up at five, if that's okay."

"All right. I look forward to it."

"Me too. See you Saturday."

As Elizabeth hung up the phone, a sense of panic set in. What would she wear? She didn't have anything appropriate. Oh, why had she agreed to this?

"What's going on, Lizzie?"

Mary had quietly come into the room and stood a few feet away. Elizabeth went over and grabbed her hand. "Oh, Mary. I just did the dumbest thing."

Mary frowned. "What do you mean?"

"That was John Marks. You know, the police officer who came here the other night?"

Mary's face lit up. "I remember. Let me guess. He called to ask you out, didn't he? Surely you said yes."

"I did, but I shouldn't have. It's like... It's like the words just jumped out of my mouth without my permission."

Mary squeezed her hand. "It's because you really want to go, Lizzie. Your heart took over your mouth. And I'm glad. I know you'll have a wonderful time."

"Oh, Mary. I have absolutely nothing to wear. And my hair..." Elizabeth reached up and ran her fingers through her straight hair.

"Those are all things we can fix, Lizzie. I'll help you with your makeup and hair, and I have the perfect outfit for you to wear. I guarantee you'll knock his socks off."

"I don't know..."

Martha, who'd been standing at the door listening, came up and put her arm around Elizabeth. "What were you wearing when you met him, Sis?"

"I...I don't remember. I guess just a plain skirt and a yellow blouse. My plain old loafers."

"Were you wearing makeup?" Mary asked.

"Not much. Just a little mascara."

"Yet he called you for a date," Martha said with a smile. "Don't you realize he already likes you? We'll help you get dolled up if that's what you want, but he asked you out based on how you looked the other night. He found you attractive just as you are. You have nothing to worry about."

The truth of what her sisters said got through to her. He *did* like her when she was dressed in her frumpiest. She liked John, and she actually wanted to go out with him. The truth chased away the tightness in her stomach. "I guess you're right. But I still want you to help me. A little more attention to my looks wouldn't hurt."

Mary laughed, and Martha hugged her.

"Let's clean up our dinner dishes," Martha said.

Elizabeth followed her sisters back into the kitchen. For the first time in days, Anita Smucker wasn't the most important person on her mind.

CHAPTER EIGHTEEN

Martha cleared the dishes while the sisters continued talking about the sword in Uriah Barnhart's possession.

"The sword has to be the valuable possession Warren was referring to in his riddle," Mary said. "Nothing else fits. There's a bird, and there's thunder."

"Well," said Elizabeth, "we don't know that for certain. What if these clues could be found hidden somewhere in the painting? That's possible."

Mary harrumphed. "Well, the sword certainly seems like the most obvious lead we've got. Don't dismiss it until we've explored the option, at least. I say let's follow this lead until we reach a dead end. Then we can move on to another possibility."

"Okay," Elizabeth said with a shrug. "Assuming you're onto something, what about the dirty pies?"

Mary bit her lower lip as she stared at her. Elizabeth could almost hear the gears turning in her sister's head.

"Mud pies," Martha said suddenly as she rinsed off a plate. She turned around to look at them. "Could dirty pies be mud pies? You know, like we used to make as kids?"

"But what does that have to do with the sword?" Mary asked.

Elizabeth shrugged. "Well…maybe it's just mud."

Mary sighed, got up, and grabbed her tablet. After typing something in, she smiled. "Here's something. A place called Mud Creek. Seems there was a battle there during the Civil War."

"Where is Mud Creek?" Martha asked.

"In Georgia."

Martha came over and sat down at the table. "Would Anita's great-great-grandfather have fought in Georgia?"

"I have no idea," Elizabeth said. "I'd love to call and ask her, but I'm not sure she'd speak to me right now."

"Even if we might be solving the riddle?" Mary asked.

"Probably not."

"Hey," Mary said, pointing at the tablet. "It seems the *Continental* Congress, back in the 1700s, prohibited slavery. The northern states accepted it, but the southern states didn't. It's what led to the Civil War."

"That's reaching a bit, isn't it?" Martha asked, doubt clearly written on her face.

Mary shook her head. "Hey, it's the only thing that fits so far." She turned off her tablet. "I'm telling you, it's the sword. It has to be."

"Maybe you're right," Elizabeth said. "Perhaps Warren's riddles were difficult because he used obscure references to make it harder for Anita to solve them." She sighed. "I'll call her tomorrow and ask her about these clues. Hopefully she won't hang up on me. If she thinks the clues point to the sword, then maybe she can figure out why it's valuable." She nodded toward Mary and Martha. "But just in case, you two need to research the sword. I'm going to do the best I can, but you know I'm not that good on the computer."

"Yeah, we learned that last winter when you got a message saying you had mail, and you put on your coat, gloves, and hat and walked out to the mailbox."

"You're never going to let me forget that, are you? I'd just gotten the computer."

Mary giggled. "Oh, Lizzie. You're always so smart and organized. We love knowing that you're fallible too. I don't like being the only dingle-head in the family."

The three women laughed. Although the incident still embarrassed Elizabeth, at least now she could see the humor in it.

"You know," Martha said, shaking her head, "even if the solution to the riddle and the thing of value is the sword, we have a whole new problem. How can we get it back from Uriah?"

"He was adamant," Elizabeth said. "It's personal with him. I have to assume he doesn't believe his ancestor killed Anita's great-great-grandfather."

"But didn't you say they were friends? Why would one friend kill another? Especially in the middle of a war. Wouldn't serving together bind them to each other even more?"

Elizabeth shrugged. "I have no idea, but I don't think we'll ever find out. It's not like they're around to tell us what happened."

"Sure would make it easier if we could talk to them," Martha said.

"No kidding," Mary said with a grin.

"Is there any kind of research we can do that might help us find the truth?" Martha asked.

Elizabeth thought for a moment. "I'm not sure. I doubt there's anything that would point exactly to what happened between the two men. It would help if we at least knew Uriah's great-great-grandfather's name."

"Ask Anita," Martha said.

"I don't suppose either one of you would like to talk to her?" Elizabeth asked with a sigh.

"What? When you've already established such a great rapport with her?" Mary said, grinning.

"Very funny."

Martha nodded at Elizabeth. "Mary might be teasing you, but she's probably right. You're the more measured sister, Lizzie. I'm too acerbic and Mary's too . . . well, Mary. It's not that we don't want to help you. It's just that you're probably the best person to deal with her."

Even though the last thing she wanted to do was confront Anita again, Elizabeth recognized her sisters were right. Martha didn't suffer fools easily, and Mary was too flippant. "I'll call her tomorrow," she said finally. "But I'm not sure what good it will do. No matter what, Uriah has no intention of giving up that sword. I'm certain of it."

"But if we find out what really happened," Martha said, "it might at least help us to understand."

"I—I guess."

"I'm going to load the dishwasher and read for a while," Martha said.

Elizabeth stood up. "I'll help you."

"You relax, Lizzie," Mary said. "I'll help Martha. You've had a tough day." She pointed to the stairs that led to the bedrooms.

"Go through my closet and look for an outfit you think would work for your date Saturday night. And don't pick something that makes you look like Grandmother Lois."

"Like you would have something like that," Martha said, laughing.

Mary winked at her. "You're right. What was I thinking?"

Elizabeth wasn't sure she wanted to wear anything of Mary's, but she was too tired to argue. She left her sisters in the kitchen and went upstairs to Mary's bedroom. When she opened the door, she wasn't surprised to find the room in comfortable disarray. Mary wasn't really a slob. She was just careless. When she got something out she would eventually put it away, but it might be the next day. Obviously this principle was at work this evening. Mary's pajamas from last night were thrown over the chair in the corner, and her makeup and hair products were scattered on the top of her dresser.

Elizabeth went over to the closet, hoping it wouldn't be a mess. Thankfully, everything was hung up neatly, and Mary's shoes were displayed in a neat line. She sorted through the clothes until she found a silky bluish-gray blouse that matched her eyes. She put it together with a pair of black pants. She slipped off her skirt and top and tried on the outfit. They fit her perfectly, and Elizabeth liked the way she looked. The clothes hugged her shape, making her appear more feminine. A pair of black pumps set the outfit off perfectly. After staring at herself in Mary's full-length mirror for a while, she decided the clothes would work for her date with John. She undressed and put her old clothes back on. A quick glance in the mirror shocked her. She looked so old and tired. When had she quit caring about how she looked? She wasn't sure, but it was clear it was time to take her life back.

She put the clothes on the bed and wandered over to the dresser. She picked up Mary's brush and tried to do something with her hair. She had dark-brown hair with reddish highlights. She liked the color but not the touches of gray that were beginning to show through.

Elizabeth took the barrettes out of her hair and let it fall down to her shoulders. Then she picked up a lipstick and applied a little to her mouth. After that, she tried some of Mary's eye shadow called Smoky Gray. She dabbed a little on her eyelids. Although she liked the effect, she realized the eye shadow made her eyelashes disappear. She picked up Mary's black mascara and lightly ran the wand over her lashes. She was surprised at the results. She didn't look quite so tired, and the eye shadow seemed to make her eyes stand out. Suddenly a voice from behind her said, "Oh, Lizzie. How pretty!"

Elizabeth jumped and spun around to find Mary standing at the door, watching her. "Heavens to Betsy, Mary. Warn me when you come into a room."

Mary smiled at Elizabeth. "You look lovely. A little finessing and it will be perfect. I'll help you on Saturday before you leave for your date."

"Thanks, Sis. I hope I'm doing the right thing. At my age—"

"You're only fifty-seven, Lizzie. That's not old."

Elizabeth took a deep breath and blew it out quickly. "Well, it feels old right now."

Mary came over and put her hand on Elizabeth's cheek for a moment. "You took care of Mama for years. You didn't get to have a life of your own. But we're here now. It's time you got out of this place and had some fun. Find yourself again."

"That's just it. I'm not sure who I am anymore." Elizabeth reached down and picked up her barrettes, pulling her hair back on the sides and snapping them in place. "It may take some time for me to find out."

Mary gave Elizabeth a small smile. "If anyone understands, it's me. I thought I was the woman Brian loved. His wife. Then suddenly I wasn't. I'm not sure who Mary is now. But one thing I do know, the Classen sisters are going to be okay. When we join together, we're a force to be reckoned with."

In spite of herself, Elizabeth laughed. "Yes, we are." She put her arms around Mary. "You're an incredible person, Mary. Someday you'll meet someone who will see what Martha and I see."

"Thanks, Lizzie. I really appreciate that." Mary squeezed Elizabeth and then let her go but not before Elizabeth saw her attempt to blink away tears. "I'm gonna make some tea and read a bit before bed. Want me to make you a cup too?"

Elizabeth shook her head. "Thanks, but I think I'll take a shower and go to bed early. I need to think about what I'm going to say to Anita tomorrow. It should be interesting."

"Okay. Good night, Sis. Love you."

Elizabeth smiled. "Love you too."

As Elizabeth headed toward her own bedroom, she began to rehearse her phone call to Anita. No matter what she came up with, it didn't sound right. "Oh, God," she prayed, "would You please give me the words to say tomorrow? I don't want to make this woman an enemy, and I don't want this situation to hurt our reputation. If we could just find the treasure Warren left for her, it would finally end this."

As she prepared for bed, Elizabeth tried to quiet her troubled mind. She felt as if she was forgetting something. No matter how hard she tried, she couldn't seem to remember what it was.

CHAPTER NINETEEN

As the sisters prepared for another day at Secondhand Blessings, they were all quiet. Even Mary didn't say much when she came in with the day's egg collection. Tinkerbelle followed her around as if she knew something was wrong.

"I didn't hear Reddy crow this morning," Martha said suddenly, breaking Elizabeth out of her reverie.

"I did," Mary said. "You must have been sleeping."

"I was tired last night," she admitted. "I stayed up late baking." She turned to face Elizabeth and Mary. "I'm not sure how much more of this I can handle."

"Maybe you could spend more time inside the house during the day," Elizabeth said. "I'm sorry I've been out so much. I realize when I'm not here you've got to back Mary up in the shop."

Martha looked relieved. "Switching some of the baking to daytime hours would be great. Maybe I could stay inside in the mornings and bake. After lunch I'll come to the shop, and if either one of you needs to leave, or just needs a break, you could do it then. Would that work?"

Mary and Elizabeth looked at each other.

"I'm fine with that," Mary said. "I've been trying to help Martha at night, and it's been wearing me out too."

"Let's try that for a while," Elizabeth said. "Hopefully, things will settle down, and I won't have to be away so much."

Martha put a plate of pancakes on the table. "Don't worry about it. None of it has been your fault."

"So, you're planning to stay here today?" Mary asked.

Elizabeth picked up the coffeepot Martha had put on the table and poured herself a cup. "That's the plan. I'll call Anita after breakfast and hope she doesn't insist I come to see her."

Martha grunted. "She shouldn't *insist* on anything. We're running a business, not just catering to her." She set a bottle of syrup next to the pancakes. "If it wasn't for the store's reputation, I'd tell her to jump in a lake. This is her fault, you know. From beginning to end."

"Well, I don't know about that," Elizabeth said. "She had no idea that her father had a fortune hidden in their house."

"But he did tell her not to sell certain things," Mary interjected, "and she did it anyway."

"That's true, but I still say whatever it is he was referring to might not even be in the stuff she gave us." Martha slammed a plate of link sausages down on the table as if emphasizing her point.

"Then why didn't the appraiser she hired find anything really valuable?"

"I have no idea," Martha said. "But what if the guy's wrong? What if he lied so he could buy the real treasure for a fraction of its worth?"

"What if he's the invisible man and plans to sneak in and steal it right out from under Anita's nose?" Elizabeth said sharply. "Conjecture won't help us. Look, for now we have to keep searching. At least until all the possibilities dry up."

"And if they do?" Mary asked. "Then what?"

"I don't know," Elizabeth said, rubbing her temples, trying to chase away a slow-building headache. "We'll just have to keep trying until that happens."

Martha walked over to the table and slid the butter dish toward the plate of pancakes. "Hate to change the subject, but what time is Billy coming over tonight?"

"I told him dinner would be at six," Mary said. "That way we'll have plenty of time to shut down the store, change clothes, and get ready for supper."

"I'll have to cut out a little early," Martha said. "I want to make sure everything's ready on time."

"What are you making?" Mary asked.

"Goulash."

Mary and Elizabeth stared at her. Elizabeth was trying to come up with a way to ask Martha to change her mind, when Martha suddenly burst out laughing.

"I'm not making goulash," she said grinning. "I got the message about goulash. I overdid it. I guess I made it so much because Mama liked it."

"It's not that we don't appreciate it," Elizabeth said. "Maybe you could just cut down the number of times you serve it."

"Yeah, to none," Mary grumbled.

Martha reached over and patted Mary's hand. "How's this? We put the goulash on the back burner for a while. If I get hungry for it, I'll make some for myself and keep it in the fridge. If either of you want some, you can help yourselves."

"Sounds great," Elizabeth said. "We both really appreciate all the cooking you do. You really don't have to do all of it, you know."

"Yes, I do. I've tasted your cooking."

Mary laughed. "I admit I'm not the best cook."

"Mama thought I was a pretty good cook," Elizabeth said. "So did Daddy."

Martha smiled at her. "You are a pretty good cook, Lizzie. Really. But I'm better. And truth be told, I love cooking for you two. When Chuck died, and I suddenly found myself cooking for one. I lost my enthusiasm for it. Now it's back. You both have certain talents, and I don't have any, really, except for cooking."

Elizabeth's mouth dropped open. "Are you serious? You're the one who handles the money. You research the value of most of the items that come in. You're the organized one. You have more talent than anyone I've ever known."

Martha blinked several times, and tears shone in her eyes. "Thank you, Lizzie. I'm not sure I deserve that much praise, but cooking for you has really been a joy for me. I'm beginning to feel more like myself. Without Chuck I've felt like half a person. A lot of the things I did weren't needed anymore. Slowly but surely, I'm finding myself again. Please don't ever think anything I do for us is a burden. It isn't. It's my salvation."

Elizabeth's voice broke as she gazed at her sisters. "I'm so glad we're all together. We're helping each other to grow stronger. I thank God every day that you both wanted to come here and open the store again. It's an answer to prayer."

"For all of us, Lizzie," Mary said.

Martha nodded. "Amen."

"Now, back to supper tonight," Mary said, wiping a tear that snaked down her cheek. "What are you really making?"

"Pot roast with potatoes, onions, and carrots. Salad with Gorgonzola cheese, walnuts, craisins, and raspberry vinaigrette. For dessert, caramel apple pie and ice cream."

The women hurriedly finished their breakfasts so they could open the store on time.

Once the store was ready to greet its first customer, Elizabeth took her cell phone and went outside where she could get a clearer signal. There was a landline in the store, but she didn't want customers overhearing her conversation.

She walked toward the front porch, said a short prayer, and then dialed Anita's number. After three rings, she answered.

"Anita, it's Elizabeth. Last night my sisters and I went over the riddle again, and I think we may have figured something out." She quickly launched into their reasons for suspecting the sword was the answer to her father's riddle. When she finished, Elizabeth took a quick breath before Anita could interrupt and said, "Did your great-great-grandfather fight in Georgia?"

There was silence from the other line for a moment. Elizabeth was just about to ask Anita if she was still there when she finally heard her voice.

"I researched the sword carefully," she said in clipped tones. "It isn't the sword."

"But we all think it fits, Anita. It's the only item we can think of right now that comes close. What if the sword was originally owned by someone else? Maybe that's what makes it special."

"But how am I supposed to figure that out?" she asked. "There's nothing that points toward the sword's original owner. My father wouldn't have given me a riddle that couldn't be solved. He wasn't cruel. *If* the sword has a famous owner, he would have left something behind to point me in that direction."

"But he was…sick," Elizabeth said gently. "Maybe he thought he did. Or maybe he did, but you just haven't realized it yet."

"I'd love to get another look at that sword," she said. "Because of its history, I never paid much attention to it."

"Perhaps Uriah would allow me to take a few pictures of it," Elizabeth said. "I could ask. Then I could bring the pictures to you so you could go over them. Maybe there's something there that would help you."

Anita was quiet for a moment. "All right," she said finally. "I guess that would work."

"Good. I'll get back with you after I see Uriah. Anita, could Uriah know something about the sword's value that you don't?"

"I can't imagine he would. He couldn't have found out more about it than I did. I showed it to my appraiser before I gave it to you. He did tell me that if it had belonged to someone famous, it would be worth more, but neither one of us had any reason to believe that was the case."

"All right. Just sit tight while I try to see Uriah again. If nothing else, I'm going to get some really good pictures. From tip to tip and on both sides."

"Thank you, Elizabeth," Anita said in muted tones. "I'm sorry I was so combative with you yesterday. You're a nice person. I'm just so frustrated with all of this. The bank is making threats, and I don't know what to do."

"I understand, Anita. It's okay."

Although she was still irritated with the woman, she knew the best way to handle things was to find a place of peace. She wasn't going to fool herself though. She realized that more bad news might push Anita back toward anger. Any truce would probably be short-lived. Elizabeth decided this was the time to act on her request for the painting.

"Anita, I met Eleanor Wallace the other day. She told me about her daughter, Kelly."

There was a long sigh from the other end of the phone. "I need to take care of that right away. I should have been kinder. I think the financial pressures felt overwhelming, and when Eleanor asked for the painting, I snapped. I'll take the painting to them today. Thank you for reminding me."

Deciding not to share the circumstances of her interaction with Eleanor, Elizabeth said, "I'm so glad. What a blessing that will be to them. In the meantime I'll visit Uriah. I certainly hope I can find out something useful."

"I pray you're right. Time is getting short. I need a resolution soon."

"I'll contact you again when I have something to show you. And if there's any way you can find out more about exactly what happened between Gideon's and Uriah's great-great-grandfathers, it might be really helpful."

Following a brief silence, Anita said, "I just remembered something. In going through the house, trying to find things to sell, I found an old trunk in the attic. My father had said it was full of old clothes, but underneath them, I found a book.

It looked like a diary. It's possible I might find something help-ful in it."

Elizabeth's heart leaped with hope. "Oh, Anita, if we could find out more about Gideon, we might find out more about the sword too. I'm convinced there's a story behind it that makes it valuable."

"I see what you mean. I've got some other things to do first, but I'll retrieve the book and go through it as soon as I can."

Elizabeth thanked her and had started to say goodbye, when Anita suddenly cleared her throat. "I know you're trying your best to help me, Elizabeth. I really am sorry for threaten-ing you. I guess I've been so afraid of losing everything that I've been lashing out at everyone. My fear is that no one will help me just because I need help. That if I intimidate them in some way, they'll be forced to help."

"That might be true in some cases, Anita, but not with us. My sisters and I will do everything we can to find your treasure because we care about you. That's our only reason, okay?"

Elizabeth could hear Anita sniff several times. She was moved with compassion for the woman and even more deter-mined to find a way to uncover the treasure she was searching for. Now it was personal.

CHAPTER TWENTY

Elizabeth worked in the shop all morning so Martha could spend time in the kitchen. After lunch Elizabeth drove over to Uriah's house, praying God would not only give her a way to find out more about the sword, but also open a door of understanding between her and the obviously lonely old man. She would have called him but still hadn't been able to locate his telephone number.

As she pulled up in front of Uriah's house, she prayed again. "I need to have some compassion for this man, Lord," she whispered. "Although I don't feel it, You're living in me. Will You help me lean on Your overwhelming love? Thank You, Lord."

By the time she reached the front porch she felt calmer. After a few knocks, the ancient door swung open a little, the hinges squealing.

"What do you want?" Uriah asked when he saw her standing there. "I thought we said everything we needed to say when you were here last."

"I thought we did too, Mr. Barnhart," Elizabeth replied, "but I have some questions about the sword. I'm not trying to get it back, I just want to know something about its history. I've talked to Anita—"

"Anita Smucker doesn't know anything about that sword," Uriah snapped back. "I'm the only one left alive who knows the truth."

"Shouldn't someone else hear what really happened? Someday when you're gone, don't you want people to know the sword's real history?"

Uriah's bushy eyebrows shot up as high as he could probably manage. "And why in the world do you think you're the person I want to leave my story with? Who are you to me?"

"Well, I'd like to be your friend, if you'd let me. I know my mother considered you a friend."

"Your mother was someone...special. Not many like her in the world."

"I agree." Elizabeth wasn't sure he was going to talk to her, so when he suddenly swung the door open the rest of the way, she was surprised...and relieved.

"Come on in. But don't make this a habit."

"Thank you. I won't." Although she wouldn't tell Uriah Barnhart, coming back to this house was the last thing she wanted to do. However, if God opened a door for her, she was willing to reach out to Uriah. It might be difficult, but she could do it for Anita's sake. Besides, Mama had seen something in the old man that she liked. Elizabeth trusted her mother's instincts. Maybe Elizabeth could discover something worthwhile about Uriah too. She started to close the door behind her when Uriah stopped her.

"Leave it open," he said. "I like to let air in through the screen door."

Frankly, Elizabeth was happy to do it. The house had a musty, closed-up smell. Fresh air could only help.

Uriah led her toward the living room. As they passed the room she'd seen before, she glanced quickly to see if the sword was in the same place. Thankfully, it was still there. Elizabeth sat down on the couch, once again carefully avoiding the protruding spring.

"So you want to know the history of the sword?" Uriah asked as he lowered himself into a chair across from her. "What do you know so far?"

Elizabeth hesitated for a moment before saying, "Anita says your great-great-grandfathers were very good friends. They fought together in the Civil War. They got into a fight, and your great-great-grandfather killed hers. With the sword."

Uriah's face turned red. "Poppycock. That's not what happened at all."

"Then what did happen?" she asked gently, trying not to arouse his volatile temper.

He leaned back in his overstuffed chair, pushing against it as if trying to find a way out of the conversation and the room itself. He took a deep breath. "Gideon Smucker and Noah Barnhart fought in the same Union battalion. They became good friends."

"Did they fight in Georgia?" Anita asked.

Uriah frowned at the interruption. "Yes, they did. Why do you ask?"

Elizabeth nervously cleared her throat. She didn't want to give away anything and make Uriah suspicious. "I just heard something about a Mud or Muddy Creek?"

"You mean the Mud Creek Line," he said. "In battle, lines are drawn, and one was drawn at Mud Creek in Georgia. I honestly have no idea if Gideon and Noah were there, but it's entirely possible." He glared at her. "May I continue?"

Elizabeth nodded.

"Anyway, one day their battalion fought Confederate troops in an especially bloody battle. During the fighting, Gideon was attacked by a rebel soldier. He was getting ready to finish Gideon off when Noah intervened. He shot the rebel before he could inflict injury on Gideon. Noah saved his life."

"Noah was a hero."

"Yes, he was. To thank him, Gideon gave him a very special sword he'd found during one of the major battles of the Civil War. Although the men weren't sure who the sword had belonged to, there were rumors it had been a gift to a very brave soldier from Stonewall Jackson. The soldier had been killed and the sword left on the battlefield before it was acquired by Gideon."

"If it really belonged to Stonewall Jackson, it could be worth a fortune."

"Sure, if it could be proven, but it never has been."

Elizabeth was so entranced by the story, for a while she'd forgotten the reason she was there. She reminded herself to get back to her real purpose. "I—I might be able to help you with that," she said. "I do research all the time on old objects."

Uriah straightened up quickly in his chair and glowered at her. "I told you I'll never give you that sword."

Elizabeth held up her hand like a cop stopping traffic. "I know. I wasn't asking for it. If I could just take pictures of it, I could do the research and let you know what I discover."

Uriah seemed to study her for a moment. "I'll think about it. But you tell me what you find out. Not Anita."

Even though Elizabeth wasn't sure she could keep that promise, she nodded at him. "It seems like Gideon and Noah would be even closer after Noah saved Gideon's life. What happened that led to Gideon's death?"

The elderly man stared down at the floor for a moment. When he raised his face, Elizabeth was surprised to see sadness in his eyes. "I can only repeat the story told to me by my grandfather." He sighed deeply, almost as if he were in pain. "They were advancing on Atlanta. Fighting was fierce and had gone into the night. It was raining. Soldiers were slipping and sliding. Noah had just finished fighting a Confederate soldier to the death when someone else came up behind him. Without thinking he swung his sword around. Unfortunately, it was Gideon. The sword pierced Gideon's chest, and he was killed. Noah was beside himself with grief."

"Oh my," Elizabeth said. "How awful. What happened to Noah?"

"He told his superior officer about the incident, but there were so many casualties and the war was almost over. He was told to keep the incident to himself. They knew it was an accident and convinced Noah that it would be better for everyone if it was assumed Gideon was killed by a Confederate soldier."

Elizabeth pondered the gravity of the story she'd just heard. Noah Barnhart must have suffered great guilt over the situation. She felt sorry for him.

Uriah grunted. "But then another soldier in Gideon's battalion went to Gideon's family and told them that Gideon and

Noah had a falling out. That Noah had murdered him for a sword rumored to have once belonged to Stonewall Jackson. The Smuckers believed him."

"But why would this soldier tell them that?"

"Who knows?" Uriah shook his head. "Jealousy, maybe. Maybe he hated Noah. Whatever the reason, the Smuckers believe that story to this day."

"How did they end up with the sword?"

"The Smuckers threatened to go to the authorities and accuse Noah of murder if he didn't give them the sword. Noah was heartbroken that his friend's family could accuse him of such treachery, and he knew he couldn't prove in a court of law that killing Gideon had been an accident. So he gave them the sword."

Uriah looked at Elizabeth, his eyes blazing. "That sword should have stayed with us. Gideon gave Noah the sword, and it should stay in this family." His voice softened. "Noah Barnhart was a hero. He saved Gideon Smucker's life. What happened later was an accident. It doesn't take anything away from Noah's heroism."

Because of what happened, Elizabeth had to wonder why the old sword mattered so much. It seemed to be nothing more than the symbol of death and anger. Unless the story about Jackson was true. Finding out who it had originally belonged to seemed to be the key to everything. She suddenly remembered the last lines of the riddle. *Open your eyes, and you'll see the truth. Hidden in shadows and very sentimental.* They seemed to fit the story of the sword perfectly. The truth of what happened had been hidden in shadows, and the sentiment was in the story of two friends whose lives were shaped by one terrible event. The sword had to be the answer to the riddle. And if Warren Smucker knew its true worth, then he obviously found a way to prove the sword belonged to Stonewall Jackson. It seemed to Elizabeth that he must have left something behind to help his daughter sell it for its full value. But where was it? If they couldn't find the proof, maybe there was something in the diary Anita mentioned. Something that would help.

Right now, everything hinged on uncovering the truth about Gideon Smucker's sword. How in the world could they do that? At that moment, Elizabeth wasn't holding out much hope.

CHAPTER TWENTY-ONE

As she continued to ponder all the possibilities, Elizabeth realized her mind had wandered and she fought to refocus.

"…Warren Smucker thought he had me," Uriah was saying. "But I outfoxed him and all the Smuckers. Anita will never get this sword back."

"I understand how you feel," Elizabeth said, "but Anita really needs—"

He waved a hand at her. "I'm not going to debate this with you. The sword is mine. I bought it fair and square, and I won't give it back. Period."

Rather than wrangle with him, Elizabeth decided to take a different tack. "Will you let me take some pictures and do research for you?"

"I've done some already and haven't found anything that proves the sword belongs to Jackson."

"But I have some sources you don't. Actual people who handle Civil War mementos." She was telling the truth. Back before her mother took ill and they had to close Secondhand Blessings, the two of them had found online research insufficient in many cases and had placed calls to several experts in antiques. She was thinking about a man in Georgia who handled pieces from the Civil War. And a friendly appraiser in California had given Elizabeth her name and phone number in case she ever needed her help. They'd never found a reason to contact her...until now.

"I guess you can take some pictures, but as I said, you tell me what you find. Not Anita Smucker."

Elizabeth turned his request over in her head. Could she do what he asked? If the sword didn't belong to Anita anymore, was Elizabeth bound to share information with her?

"Are you having a hard time agreeing to my request?" Uriah asked finally, his face screwed up in a tight scowl.

Elizabeth took a deep breath. "I am. I want to say yes, but I'm not sure I can." She paused for a second or two. "What if I promise to tell you first? Since Anita sent me to try and buy the sword back, I don't think I can lie to her about its value if I discover something important that affects its worth. If I can't find anything, I won't bring up my search. But if I do..."

Uriah shrugged. "If you find out that the sword belonged to Jackson you must tell me first. You can share it with Anita Smucker after that. Just give me a week to decide what to do. I might put it up for auction."

Elizabeth was surprised by his change of tune, but it didn't take long to find out why he'd done an about-face.

"Let her know what she missed out on. That won't bother me at all."

"But I thought you wanted to keep the sword in the family. Why would you sell it?"

Uriah's expression hardened even more. "Because if it goes to auction, everyone will hear the truth about what happened.

About Noah Barnhart's bravery. The Smuckers will never be able to throw stones at him again."

Although Elizabeth wasn't certain about that, she felt it was best to leave well enough alone at this point. At least she would be able to tell Anita the truth.

"All right. I'll do as you ask," she said.

Uriah got to his feet. "Follow me. I'll show you the sword."

She followed him to the adjoining room where the sword lay on the buffet. The rest of the room seemed to be used for storage. There were many fine pieces of furniture pushed against the walls. Probably some valuable antiques. She could only guess that the room had once been used as a study or library. Bookshelves lined two of the walls, and a massive desk sat in a corner. Over the years, it seemed other belongings had been relegated to the room. It was packed with all kinds of junk. Too bad. The room was charming with its tall windows, oak wainscoting, and crown molding.

Although she'd seen the sword before, this time Elizabeth looked at it more closely. It was obviously old, and even though it wasn't in pristine condition, she would say it was in pretty good shape.

"This was one of Jackson's extra swords," Uriah said. "He had another he carried with him. When he died, they found that sword rusted because he rarely used it." He shrugged. "Maybe he used this one more, I have no idea."

Uriah lifted the sword and held it up so Elizabeth could take pictures. The hilt was intricate, a carved eagle holding something in his talons. But when she looked closer, they seemed more like arrows than thunderbolts. Had Warren made a mistake in his riddle?

After a few more pictures, Elizabeth thanked Uriah for seeing her and promised to get back to him. When she left, she almost closed the front door, but at the last second, she remembered to leave it open. Then she nearly tripped over a couple of bottles of milk right in front of the door and came close to putting her foot through a hole in the porch. She had to watch her step to make it off the porch safely. Visiting Uriah could be dangerous in more ways than one.

On the way home, she couldn't help pondering the arrows. Had they been wrong about the sword? Was it possible it wasn't the valuable piece they were looking for? She'd gone from being positive she'd solved the riddle to confusion. She couldn't throw out all the rest of the evidence pointing to it, but the arrows bothered her. They weren't thunderbolts, and that was pretty easy to see. Maybe Warren had bad eyesight. She'd check on that, but still, she felt he would have known the difference.

Elizabeth had one more stop to make before going home. Her old purse was falling apart. Even though she didn't fuss much with purses, she wanted something nice to carry on her date with John. She drove to Hickory Acres Crafts to buy a new bag. They sold the Amish-made cloth bags she loved so much. It only took her a few minutes to settle on a lovely dark-blue bag with a small pattern. She liked the more colorful bags, but she felt the need for something a little more understated with John.

After she left the shop, she started to turn onto the road that led back to the Classen farm, but at the last second she turned the other way, down North Ronks Road. Dottie Spencer ran a beauty shop out of her home. She'd taken care of Elizabeth's hair for several years. Dottie had encouraged her to try a more modern cut for some time. Dottie also wanted to color her hair.

"Your hair is so nice," she'd say to Elizabeth. "But you don't do anything with it. A cute cut and style would really change the way you look."

Each time, Elizabeth had asked her just to cut her hair so it would stay off her shoulders. She pulled up to Dottie's, certain this was a bad idea, since Dottie only had one chair and required appointments, but Elizabeth couldn't stop herself from getting out of the car and knocking on the door. When Dottie answered, she looked surprised.

"I know you're probably busy," Elizabeth said, feeling flustered and foolish. "But I was thinking about what you said. You know, about my hair? And—"

Dottie's sculpted eyebrows shot up, and she smiled, her green eyes sparkling. "So today's the day? You're ready to take a chance?" She swung the door open, her curly red hair bouncing as if it were as excited as its owner. "I don't have anyone today. We have plenty of time."

For just a moment, Elizabeth almost backed out. But instead, she squared her shoulders and walked inside. "Yes, I'm ready. Let's do it."

CHAPTER TWENTY-TWO

Mary spent the day thinking about Billy Richmond. He would actually be at the house tonight. She would get to see him in a more casual environment. Although she'd known him for years, they'd never really been close, even though they'd gone to all the same schools. She'd never missed a high school football game if she could help it, and cheered Billy on as he ran for many a touchdown for the Buckskins in his senior year. She'd thought he was cute, but he was three years older than she was—a lot of difference when you're a kid. Not that much when you get older.

Even though she knew her sisters would be with her, she was still nervous. What should she wear? Should she use perfume? Should she dress casually, or should she wear something fancy? What would they talk about? She considered how she'd feel if he asked about her divorce. Surprisingly, she realized it wouldn't bother her. Probably because she knew his question would be out of concern for her—not out of idle curiosity.

The afternoon was a little slow, so when Martha suggested they close early, Mary quickly agreed.

"I need to get started on supper," Martha said. "And it wouldn't hurt to do a little cleaning before Billy comes."

"I'll dust the living room and sweep," Mary said.

"That would be great. And maybe if you..."

The words faded when Mary saw Elizabeth walk through the door. Her hair! Instead of hanging limp, it was bouncy, had some curl, and was styled in a casual but cute way. The gray had been covered, but it was so close to her real color that it looked completely natural. Her eyebrows had been trimmed, and she wore some light makeup. She looked like Elizabeth...but younger and more vibrant. At that moment, Mary realized the color in Elizabeth's cheeks wasn't just makeup. She was embarrassed.

"Oh, Lizzie," Mary said, "you...you look lovely."

Elizabeth blinked several times and nervously touched her hair. "Are you sure I don't look silly? I don't want to come off as some old lady trying to be young."

Martha snorted. "For Pete's sake, Lizzie. You're hardly an old lady. And you look gorgeous. If you didn't, we'd tell you. We're your sisters. We'd never allow you to look silly."

Elizabeth's expression softened noticeably. "I believe you. I—I like it. I just don't want John to think I'm trying too hard."

Mary shook her head. "He won't, Sis. You look like someone who's going out on a date. Almost every woman fixes herself up a bit when she's going out. Quit worrying. You look awesome."

"You're going to have to use the curling iron to keep that style," Martha said.

"I might need help with that."

Mary held up her hand as if volunteering. "I'd be happy to help you. It won't be that hard. You'll be able to do it yourself after I show you once."

Elizabeth looked around the empty shop. "Since we're not busy, why don't we close up so we can get ready for Billy?"

Martha laughed. "Good idea. Why didn't we think of it?"

The women quickly gathered their money and receipts and headed into the house. Mary was grateful the attention was focused on Elizabeth. Right now she felt like Mexican jumping beans were having a festival in her stomach. Why was she so nervous? It was ridiculous. Billy was a friend. She should be relaxed. Why wasn't she?

As they cleaned up and Martha started supper, Elizabeth shared her experiences at Uriah's house.

"So the eagle was holding arrows in his talons?" Mary said. "Not thunderbolts? Could Warren have made a mistake?"

"With a sword he'd had for years?" Martha asked. "Doesn't make sense."

"But what else could it be?" Elizabeth said with a sigh. "I was so sure it had to be the sword. Where do we look now?"

"This is getting ridiculous," Martha said. "When do we say enough is enough?"

Elizabeth, who was making the salad while Martha worked on the main meal, shook her head. "I honestly don't know. We started out trying to keep Anita from ruining our store, but now I feel sorry for her. When she said she was taking the painting over to Kelly Wallace's house, I wanted to help her find her treasure just because—"

"Just because you wanted to help her," Mary said. She'd set the table, dusted, and swept the living room and was ready to change for dinner. "I have an idea. Let's take the night off and enjoy ourselves. I'm tired of thinking about

Anita and her so-called *treasure*. How about we find another topic tonight?"

"I'm with you," Elizabeth said with a smile.

"Me too," Martha called out.

Mary looked at the dogs and the cat assembled in the kitchen, each one hoping someone would accidentally drop food on the floor. "Come on, you mangy critters. Let's get you all fed. Then maybe you'll leave us alone for a while."

"I'll do it, Mary," Elizabeth said. "It's my job."

"Don't worry about it. I like doing it. You've been running all day. Let me help."

Elizabeth smiled. "Thanks. I really appreciate that. I am a little tired."

Mary walked to the mudroom in the back of the house where Tink's and Butterscotch's food bowls were kept. Pal couldn't eat with them because if given the chance, he'd scarf up everyone's food. Mary filled a bowl for Tink, who was dancing on his hind legs in his excitement and for Butterscotch, who was winding around her legs. After they settled at their bowls, she left the mudroom, shutting the door behind her so Pal couldn't bother them while she got his food ready. After getting him taken care of, she went back inside and hurried to her bedroom. She stood in front of her closet, staring, still not sure what to wear.

"Do you want us to dress up?"

Mary whirled around to see Elizabeth standing in her doorway. "We don't want to embarrass you. Dressy or casual?"

Mary laughed. "The exact question I was just asking myself."

"Can I offer some advice?"

Mary nodded.

"I realize I'm probably the last person who should advise anyone about fashion, but I suspect Billy will dress casually since we just asked him to supper. I mean, it's not like we're going out to a fancy restaurant."

Mary breathed a deep sigh of relief. "You're right." She plopped down on her bed. "Why am I so nervous about this? I'm not sure if it's because I like him or because I'm afraid he likes me. He's a wonderful man. But I really don't think I'm ready to get involved with anyone yet."

Elizabeth came over and sat down next to her, taking her hands. "Why don't you talk to Billy about it, Mary? Just be friends. And if he asks you, tell him the truth. What you just told me. Let him decide if he's willing to move the relationship at your pace, if you ever feel comfortable with it going beyond friendship. He might be. And if he's not…"

"I won't be able to mess up his life."

Elizabeth smiled. "*You* could never mess up anyone's life. You're a blessing. And a real catch, by the way." She let go of Mary's hands and got up. After browsing through Mary's closet, she pulled out a nice pair of jeans and a green shirt with white piping. "This green always brings out your eyes. Makes them sparkle like emeralds."

Mary laughed. "I think you're being overdramatic, but I'll take your advice. I do like this blouse." She stared at her sister for a moment before saying, "Thanks, Lizzie. Really. I—I don't know what I'd do without you and Martha."

"You'd be fine. You're a fighter, Mary. You always have been. I've always admired that about you."

"Daddy used to say I needed to pick my battles more carefully. That sometimes I attack things I should leave alone."

Elizabeth shrugged. "That might be true, but it's better to fight back than to lie down and accept everything that comes your way. Unfortunately, that's been my mistake." She walked away from the closet and headed toward the door. Before she left, she turned around and smiled at her sister again. "You're helping me too. More than you know. Now get ready. We're going to have a lovely evening. I can feel it in my bones."

As Elizabeth left the room, Mary realized there were tears in her eyes. She'd been afraid for five years. It was time to change things. Maybe tonight would be the beginning.

CHAPTER TWENTY-THREE

Elizabeth had just finished setting the table when the front doorbell rang. Billy was right on time. She glanced over at Mary, who was checking the rolls. She seemed calm. Anyway, Elizabeth hoped she was.

Elizabeth went to the front door and opened it to find Billy standing on the porch, smiling. He was a handsome man, but tonight he looked especially attractive. A blue checked shirt open at the neck set off his dark hair and brown eyes. He wore dark blue jeans and black tennis shoes. When he smiled, Elizabeth noticed how his suntanned face made his perfect teeth seem even whiter.

"Hope I'm not early," he said.

"No, you're right on time. Come on in." Elizabeth noticed he held something in his hands. He offered it to her.

"I stopped by King's Kreamery in Lancaster and picked up some of their Peanut Butter Swirl ice cream. I remembered that you all really like it. If you already have dessert planned for tonight, you can stick it in the freezer and eat it later."

Elizabeth smiled at him. Peanut Butter Swirl was Mary's favorite, and everything from King's was delicious. "Thank you, Billy. You really didn't need to do that."

"Least I could do, since you're feeding me."

Billy came inside the house and followed Elizabeth to the kitchen where Martha and Mary were putting the last touches on dinner. As they greeted him, Elizabeth handed the ice cream to Mary.

"Peanut Butter Swirl from King's," she said. Her eyes widened, and she grinned. "My favorite ice cream? Thanks, Billy."

He nodded at her, a shy smile on his face. "You're very welcome."

"I think we can sit down," Martha said. "Everything's ready." She picked up a large platter and placed it in the center of the kitchen table. The roast looked awesome. It was surrounded by perfectly roasted potatoes, carrots, and pearl onions.

"Wow," Billy said. "That looks delicious."

Loud, high-pitched barking came from somewhere in the back of the house. Tink must've smelled the roast.

"Heavens to Betsy!" Mary exclaimed. "I forgot to let Tink and Butterscotch out of the mudroom."

"Oh, Mary," Elizabeth said. "I hope they haven't made a mess."

Both women hurried to the mudroom. Fortunately, there were no accidents. The cat shot out of the room, headed straight for Martha's room. But Tinkerbelle went directly to the side door, wanting to be let out.

"You get back to the kitchen, Mary," Elizabeth said. "I'll take Tink out and watch her."

"I'm sorry, Lizzie. I guess my head was somewhere else."

Elizabeth smiled at her. "It's not a problem. Now, if any of them had left behind an unwelcome gift, it might be different."

"Well, thanks anyway."

"You're welcome."

Elizabeth followed Mary back to where Martha and Billy sat waiting at the table. "Please, go ahead," she told them. "I've got to let Tink out. I'll be back in a few minutes."

She opened the door and let Tinkerbelle outside. Tink did her business and came right back. Pal heard the commotion and joined him on the porch. Elizabeth opened the door and let both of them inside. They immediately headed under the table, waiting for scraps of food.

"I told you not to wait," Elizabeth said when she came in and found that no one was eating.

"You may have noticed that we don't always do what we're told," Martha said with a sniff.

"Yes, I have noticed that. And may I say, it's very annoying." She winked at Billy, who laughed.

"Would you like to say grace?" Martha asked him.

Billy bowed his head and prayed a beautiful prayer, thanking God for special friends and good food. Elizabeth peeked through one eye as he prayed and saw Mary watching him.

After the prayer, everyone helped themselves to Martha's top-notch dinner. The roast beef was tender and flavorful, and the roasted veggies were perfectly cooked.

"This is incredible," Billy said after swallowing a forkful of roast. "I don't get many home-cooked meals anymore."

"Thank you. After Chuck died I couldn't stand cooking for myself. Ate canned soups and stews—and frozen dinners. Being here with my sisters has ignited my desire to get into the kitchen again."

"Mary and I are glad you're having fun," Elizabeth said with a smirk. "Of course, you realize we're just eating your food because we don't want to hurt your feelings."

Martha grunted. "And I really appreciate that. What would I do without you two?"

"Have a lot more time?" Mary interjected.

Martha laughed. "Now that's certainly true."

Elizabeth had been watching Mary, hoping she would loosen up a little. Maybe Billy didn't notice, but Elizabeth could clearly see that Mary was nervous. She decided to change the subject to something that might get Mary's mind off herself. "We love the counter you made for us," she said to Billy. "It's just perfect. And all the shelves inside are great. We have plenty of room for all our supplies."

"I'm really glad you like it,'" he said. "I almost asked you about it before I started, but I knew what you'd say."

Elizabeth looked at him in surprise. "I don't understand. What would we have said?"

"You would have said it was too much trouble. That you wouldn't feel right taking it for nothing. Then you'd probably try to pay me for it."

"I don't think—" That's as far as Elizabeth got before she saw Martha and Mary nodding in agreement.

"You do that all the time, Sis," Martha said. "You're always afraid of taking advantage of someone. But people have brains, dear sister. When someone wants to bless you, you should receive it. Not question it. And you certainly shouldn't turn down blessings."

Elizabeth put her fork down and raised her hands in surrender. "You're right. I don't mean to do that. I guess after Mama died I just didn't want to feel like such a drain on our friends and family members."

"We know that, Lizzie," Martha said, "but sometimes God uses people to bless others. And then He blesses them."

"Then He has a lot of people in Bird-in-Hand to bless. They rallied around me when Mama was sick. I don't know what I would have done without them."

"I'm sorry we weren't more available," Mary said.

"Oh my goodness," Elizabeth said quickly. "I know you did everything you could. You came out here any chance you could get, and you called constantly. Please don't think I meant anything by that." She smiled at them. "You were both very supportive." She looked at Billy. "Sorry to be talking about family business in front of you."

Billy shook his head. "Not a problem. I like hearing you all talk to each other. I never had a sibling, so I get to live vicariously through you."

"Well, in my opinion, you're already part of the family," Martha said. "We can never thank you enough for everything you did for Mama and Elizabeth."

"I was honored." He took a sip of coffee, then put the cup down. "So how is everything going? I mean with the shop?"

"We have a lot of customers," Elizabeth said. "We are sure keeping busy."

Mary shook her head and sighed. "But Anita Smucker is certainly making things difficult."

Elizabeth shot her a quick look. She didn't think it was appropriate to talk about their situation in front of Billy. Mary didn't seem to notice her.

"Have you heard what's going on?" Mary asked him.

Billy colored slightly. "People are talking about it some. That you've asked anyone who bought things from Anita to bring them back."

Elizabeth shook her head. Obviously keeping this to themselves wasn't an option. But as Martha said, Billy really was like a member of the family. Maybe it was okay. "Have they mentioned why?" she asked him.

"I don't know. To be honest, I try to stay away from conversations that feel like gossip."

Elizabeth saw Martha give her a slight nod, so she briefly told Billy about the valuable item Anita was looking for. As she spoke, Billy looked more and more surprised. She wondered why. When she finished, he seemed distinctly uncomfortable. Her sisters clearly noticed it too.

"Is something wrong?" Martha asked.

Billy looked down at his plate for a moment. When he raised his head, Elizabeth could see the conflict on his face. "I—I did quite a bit of work for Warren Smucker. Some remodeling. Some repair work."

"I don't understand what that has to do with this situation," Elizabeth said.

"When the work was done, he couldn't pay for it. I told him he could pay it off as he could. Not to worry about it. But Warren didn't like to owe anyone anything. About two weeks after we talked he showed up at the shop and paid the entire bill. When I told him again it wasn't necessary, he said..." Billy took a deep breath. "He said he'd had some special possession. Something valuable. That he sold it to pay me."

Elizabeth frowned at him. "But that might have nothing to do with what Anita's searching for. It could be something totally different."

Billy nodded. "I understand that. But then he told me that he had nothing left that was worth much." He shook his head. "If he really had some kind of...treasure, why would he say that?"

CHAPTER TWENTY-FOUR

Elizabeth stared at Billy as she tried to make sense of what he'd just shared. Were they going through all of this for nothing?

"But why would he leave the riddle behind if there wasn't a reason to?" Mary asked.

"He got sick right after that," Billy said. "Maybe he never had the chance to get rid of the riddle." Billy's forehead wrinkled in thought. "Do you know how Anita found out about this...treasure?"

"She found a letter in the family Bible," Elizabeth said. "The letter told her about the treasure and contained the riddle."

"If this letter was so important, would Warren have taken a chance his daughter would stumble across it in a Bible?"

"That really does seem strange, doesn't it?" Mary asked slowly. She frowned at Billy. "Did you notice anything odd about Warren toward the end of his life? We were told he was having...problems. With dementia."

Billy nodded. "He would forget things he already told me. Get confused. I could tell he was struggling."

Martha let out a deep sigh. "This is exactly what I've been afraid of. That this whole *treasure hunt* is bogus." She shook her head. "Did Warren happen to mention whether or not he told Anita that he'd sold...whatever this was?"

"I'm sure he didn't. In fact, I wondered more than once whether I should mention it to her. In the end, I decided to mind my own business. I hope that wasn't a mistake."

"I don't suppose you know *where* he sold it, do you?" Elizabeth asked.

"No. He mentioned going to Lancaster. I suspect he took it there since it's larger and there are more places interested in buying antiques."

"But something doesn't make sense," Elizabeth said. "If this item was really so valuable, why wouldn't Warren take it to auction? And why doesn't Anita have any money now? Why does she need to live off of what we sold in the store?"

"You're right," Mary said. "That's confusing."

"He couldn't have changed his mind," Martha said, "because he paid you, Billy. So he had the money, right?"

He nodded. "But maybe we're talking about two different things here. I mean, would Warren really tell me that he had something extremely valuable? We weren't close. I barely knew him."

Mary nodded. "That must be it. Whatever he sold to pay you isn't the treasure he told Anita about. How could it be? He told her the item was worth more than everything else put together."

"Maybe." Elizabeth rubbed her forehead. The situation with Anita was already stressful. Now they had another rabbit trail to follow.

"So what should we do?" Martha asked. "Tell Anita what Billy said and see if she knows about it? If she does, we're still looking for whatever Warren wanted her to find. If not…"

"If not, we might be telling her the treasure is gone," Mary said.

Martha grunted. "And the money Warren got from it as well. Not really a conversation I want to have with her."

"Me neither," Elizabeth said. "Maybe we should just keep this to ourselves. Let me research the sword first. See if I can find out anything about it. If it turns out to be worth a lot of money, we've solved the riddle."

"But that still doesn't give it to Anita," Martha pointed out once again.

"I'm aware of that. Anita might be angry about it, but at some point she needs to take responsibility for her own actions. She's the one who gave it to us and told us to sell it. Frankly, I'm about at the end of my rope." Elizabeth realized she'd raised her voice without meaning to. "I'm sorry," she said to Billy. "We've been dealing with this since Monday. The first day we officially opened. It's been very difficult."

"If I can do anything to help…"

"Thank you, but I doubt you can. If you remember anything else Warren might have said that could have something to do with this, will you let us know?"

"Of course, but right now I can't think of anything else. We really didn't talk much."

"If I feel the need, is it okay if I tell Anita what you told us?"

Billy nodded. "Of course. I'm not trying to hide it. At the time I just felt I should stay out of it."

"Which was wise, trust us," Martha said, making a face.

"Well, let's change the subject," Mary said forcefully. "I thought we'd agreed we would take a break from all this riddle business. I'm tired of thinking about Anita."

"I agree," Martha said, rather charitably, Elizabeth thought. After all, Mary was the one who'd brought up the subject in the first place. "How about more roast, Billy?"

He smiled and shook his head. "Thank you, but I think I'll save some room for dessert if it's okay."

"It's fine. Is everyone ready now?"

Billy paused for a moment before answering. "I wonder if I could ask you ladies a favor."

"Sure," Mary said. "What is it?"

"I know when we were growing up everyone called me Billy. But…well, now I actually prefer to go by Bill. Would it be an imposition to ask you to call me Bill? I feel like a little kid around you all when you call me Billy."

"It's my fault," Elizabeth said, embarrassed. "I didn't know. I mean, I've always called you Billy. Why didn't you say something?"

"When your mother was sick?" He shook his head. "I couldn't do that. And it's all right. Really. Not a big deal. It's just…"

Although he didn't say anything else, Elizabeth saw him sneak a look at Mary. It was probably even harder being called by a nickname he associated with his childhood—a boy's name— when he was interested in a woman. Actually, Elizabeth found it endearing. She already loved Billy like a brother. This made her appreciate him even more. She picked up her clean dinner knife, walked around the table, and touched it to his shoulder.

"I dub you...Sir Bill. Nevermore to be known as Billy." Everyone laughed as she went back to her seat.

"So...Bill," Martha said. "Dessert now or later?"

He shrugged. "Either way is fine with me. What does everyone else want?"

"I think we should have dessert now," Mary said. "So we have plenty of time for...You know."

"I—I'm sorry. Did you have something planned?" Bill said.

Elizabeth nodded. "We do." She cleared her throat, surprised to find herself feeling emotional. "Bill, we have something for you. Something we hope you'll like. But if you don't want them, please let us know. The last thing we want to do is to make you feel obligated—"

"Oh for crying out loud," Mary said, interrupting. "We'd like to give you our father's tools. Since you worked with him so often, we thought you might like to have them."

Although Elizabeth was miffed that Mary had taken over and told him about the tools, the expression on his face chased away any annoyance. His mouth had dropped open, and his eyes were wide with surprise.

"What? I mean...Are you sure? What if you need them?"

Mary laughed. "We don't need Daddy's old tools. We have you."

Elizabeth sighed. "No strings attached, Billy... I mean Bill."

"That's not what I meant," Mary said. "I mean that you are the person we call when we need something fixed. Why do we need those tools?"

"I'm beyond touched," Bill said, his voice husky. "And it would be an honor to own your father's tools. Thank you so much."

"We're glad," Elizabeth said. "They're a little too heavy for us to carry upstairs. Maybe you could get them? Doesn't have to be tonight. Whenever it's convenient."

"I'd be happy to do that." He grinned at Martha. "Maybe after your delicious dessert?"

"How do you know it's delicious?" Martha asked. "You don't even know what it is yet."

Bill chuckled. "Everything you make is delicious. It's a pretty sure bet this will be too."

"It's her caramel apple pie," Mary whispered loudly. "It's terrible. I'll eat your piece if you want me to. From the goodness of my heart."

"No way," he said laughing. "I think you're lying."

Mary tried to look innocent. "I would never do that."

"Oh sure," Martha said. "Just like the time you told me Mama's raisin cookies had bugs so I wouldn't touch them."

"I was eight years old," Mary said, shaking her head. "Are you ever going to forget that?"

"Not likely." Martha got up and went to the counter for the pie, still warm from the oven. "How about some ice cream with your pie?" she asked Bill, who was clearly amused by the exchange between Martha and Mary.

"Yes, please," he said.

"How about you, Lizzie?"

"I would love some, but can I take it with me?" She smiled at Bill. "I apologize, but I have some work to do tonight. Research on a sword that Warren Smucker owned. Right now, it's in the lead in terms of our prospects for something possibly valuable. Maybe I can prove it either way."

"Sure, don't worry about it," Bill said. "I'm sure I'll be fine out here."

Martha put a plate with pie and ice cream in front of him. "You'll have to excuse me too, I'm afraid. I haven't gone over the receipts from today."

Bill looked down and stabbed at his pie, not saying anything. It was clear he was embarrassed.

Mary put her hand on his arm. "We'll be fine. Let's have dessert, and then we can take a look through our DVDs. I'll bet we can find a movie we'd both like. Is that okay with you, Bill?"

He raised his head and looked at her. Whatever he saw in her face seemed to relax him. He nodded. "Sure. That sounds great. I haven't seen a really good movie in a while."

"Then it's settled." Martha handed plates of pie and ice cream to Mary and Elizabeth.

"Thanks for coming over," Elizabeth said to Bill. "Sorry about having to scoot out early. I hope you'll come back when Martha and I don't have to work."

"I'd love to," he said. "Anytime."

As Elizabeth left the kitchen, she snuck a quick look back at Bill and Mary. What she saw on their faces made her smile.

CHAPTER TWENTY-FIVE

Although she worked for hours, Elizabeth could find nothing about the sword that led her to believe it had once been owned by Stonewall Jackson. There were many pictures of Jackson's sword, but it was different than the one in Uriah Barnhart's possession. Of course, leaders like Jackson usually had more than one sword or one gun. The fact that Jackson's regular sword was in a museum didn't rule out that the other sword was also his. However, she couldn't help but wonder if a secondary sword would have great value.

She did learn that, as Uriah had said, the sword Jackson usually wore was rusted because it was rarely used. Maybe he was more skilled with a gun. Frankly, Elizabeth would prefer a gun to a sword as well, though the idea of using either on a human being was unsettling to say the least.

She finally reached a dead end and gave up. Although she wasn't as proficient on the computer as Mary and Martha, she felt she had done a pretty good job. Before getting ready for bed she went downstairs and into the kitchen to make a cup of hot chamomile tea. When she checked the living room, she saw Bill and Mary deep in conversation.

The movie must have ended at least an hour earlier. It was a good sign.

The next morning Mary seemed especially buoyant, but Elizabeth didn't get a chance to ask her about the night before until Mary came back from taking care of the outside animals.

"Six eggs today," she announced when she came inside. "And Wynken seems a little bit off his food."

The three pygmy goats were named Wynken, Blynken, and Nod. Their mother had gotten the names from the "Dutch Lullaby," an old poem for children, which she used to recite to the three of them as she tucked them into bed at night after prayers. They had once been owned by a small petting zoo that had closed. When she heard the goats might be put down, Mama had attached the trailer to her truck and headed over there. A couple of hours later she was the proud owner of three pygmy goats. They were sweet little things who seemed to keep themselves amused, but the sisters liked spending time with them when they could.

"Do we need to call Dr. Goodrich?" Elizabeth asked.

"Not yet. But if he doesn't start eating soon, we might have to."

"He's not eating at all?" Martha asked.

"Some. But you know what a pig he is, normally. Now he's just nibbling a little. Then he walks away from the bowl."

Elizabeth looked out the window, concerned about the little goat. What she saw made her laugh. "I think I know what the problem is," she said, pointing outside.

Mary joined her at the window. Every time Wynken approached the big bowl of food, Nod nipped at him.

"Why, that little troublemaker," Mary said. She went to the cabinet and found another large metal bowl. After getting permission from Martha to take it, she went back outside and filled it with food. She gave it to Wynken, who took a few tentative bites, watching Nod with one eye. Once he felt secure, he dived into the food, eating as fast as he could. Nod tried to approach once, but Mary chastised her, and the little white goat slunk away. Elizabeth couldn't help but be amused by the trio. Especially Blynken, who seemed completely oblivious to the drama between his friends.

"I noticed you and Bill talked for quite a while last night," Elizabeth said to Mary when she came in the house.

She smiled. "Yeah, we did. It was great. We have so much in common. More than I realized."

Elizabeth snuck a look at Martha, who was listening with obvious interest. "So are you two…more than just friends?"

The smile immediately slipped from Mary's face. "No. He seemed interested in moving our relationship to more than that of friends, but I told him I just wasn't ready to think about romance yet. I think he understood."

"He may not understand forever, Mary," Martha said. "It's been five years."

"I know how long it's been," Mary snapped. She shook her head and sighed audibly. "I'm sorry, Sis. I don't know what's wrong with me. I want to agree, but I just can't."

"It's all right," Elizabeth said soothingly. "You need to wait until you're sure." She leaned over and gave Mary a hug. "We're here for you if you need us."

Mary hugged her back. "I know that. Thank you."

Although Elizabeth was sad, she didn't want Mary to make a move before she was ready. It would only make things worse.

The sisters opened the shop at ten o'clock. Martha put out the baked goods she'd made the day before and went back into the house to prepare for Monday. The sisters had talked about baking Sunday night but decided that they all needed one day off for church and rest.

Around ten thirty cars started pulling in, and Secondhand Blessings had the best sales day of the entire week. Elizabeth stayed busy and had very little time to think about Anita and the sword. When she went inside for lunch, Martha was just taking her last batch of cookies from the oven.

"Is it that time already?" she asked.

Elizabeth looked at the loaves of bread, the trays of cookies, and the cakes lined up on the kitchen counters. "You accomplished all of this? That's amazing, Martha."

Martha smiled and took off her apron. "I'll be back in a bit when everything cools off to package it." She paused and stared at Elizabeth. "Are you going to call Anita?"

Elizabeth plopped down in one of the kitchen chairs. "Don't have a choice. I didn't find anything out about the sword last night. But before I contact her I'm going to call a couple of people. Remember the guy who sells Civil War memorabilia in Georgia? I'd like to know what he thinks about this sword. And Noelle Winters in California. She knows everything about everything. If that sword is valuable, they should be able to tell me."

"And if they don't think it's worth much?"

Elizabeth shook her head. "Then I have to tell Anita. And I have to ask her if Warren could have sold something else before he died. I'll tell her I heard from someone else that he did."

"Are you going to tell her it was Billy...I mean, Bill?"

"It's going to take some time to get used to that, isn't it?"

Martha nodded.

"I probably will. He said it was okay."

"I just don't want Anita to start causing him trouble."

"Yes, I agree," Elizabeth said. "But if I don't tell her where I heard it, won't it sound suspicious?"

"I guess so. By the way, Mary and I have been searching online for information. We're not coming up with anything."

"Me either. Thanks for trying." She leaned back in her chair. "Well, let me make the other calls. Then we'll see. You might pray for me if you think of it."

Martha smiled. "I pray for you all the time, Lizzie. Don't worry about that."

"Thanks."

After Martha left, Elizabeth got her phone and her directory so she could look up the numbers she needed. A couple of minutes later she was talking to George Tyson in

Atlanta. After describing the sword and relating the story about Stonewall Jackson, she asked if he knew of any way she could attribute the Smucker sword to the Confederate general.

"I'm sorry, Miss Classen," he said in his slow Southern drawl. "This is a new one on me. It's true that soldiers had other swords and guns besides the ones they normally wore, but I've never actually seen anything about Jackson's reserve artillery." He paused for a moment. "Can you send me a picture of the sword?"

"Yes, I can email it to you right now."

Elizabeth wrote a short note, attached the pictures to the email, and sent it to George. As he waited to receive it, he asked about Secondhand Blessings.

"We're doing well, but of course it's only been a week. We have so much to learn. We hope to grow as time goes on."

"Well, if y'all get any more Civil War stuff, you know who to call."

"We'll certainly let you know."

"I'm lookin' at the picture now," he said. "Pretty typical sword from the period. Looks to be in fairly good shape."

"What do you think it's worth?"

"I'd ask about four hundred for it. What did you sell it for?"

Elizabeth gulped before saying, "A hundred dollars."

George, being a Southern gentleman, didn't chastise her. "Well, that's an excellent deal."

"George, if it could be proven, you know, that Jackson owned this sword, what would it be worth?"

"Hard to tell. His main sword is in a museum in Richmond, Virginia. If it were for sale, it would be worth a great deal. But since it's not, I can't give you a value. His extra sword? It would depend on several things. For example, did he actually use it? Can the provenance be proven? If so... Well, I hate to hazard a guess, but with solid proof, I'd think it could go for quite a lot to a collector."

"But only with proof."

"That's right. Sorry. I wish I could give you more information."

"That's okay. I really appreciate it. Will you send me a bill for your time?"

"I don't think I helped you much. Why don't you just let this be my contribution to your new endeavor?"

Elizabeth thanked him profusely and hung up. A call to Noelle Winters gave her similar information.

"It's so hard to tell," Noelle said. "Unless you can provide some kind of documentation that shows the sword actually belonged to Jackson and that he used it, it's just not worth much."

By the time Elizabeth hung up, she was pretty discouraged. She was still hopeful the sword was Warren's treasure, but unless they could prove it belonged to Stonewall Jackson, it was almost worthless. She couldn't understand how Warren could leave something so valuable to his daughter without providing her what she would need to confirm its authenticity. It seemed incredibly thoughtless.

Elizabeth finished her lunch, knowing she needed to call Anita but dreading it. They'd done everything they could to find a connection to Jackson, but they were at a dead end. Of course, even if they could find a way to tie it to the famous Confederate general, Uriah Barnhart had the sword and was determined to keep it. No matter what, it seemed that Anita was out of luck. That she'd never have the treasure her father left for her. Finally, Elizabeth decided to get it over with and dialed Anita's phone number. After several rings no one picked up so Elizabeth hung up. It wasn't her fault if Anita wasn't home, she reasoned. She decided to put off trying again until Monday. For now, she needed to concentrate on work and on her date tonight.

As she walked out the front door, headed for the barn, she tried to put Anita Smucker and her missing treasure out of her mind. But could she?

CHAPTER TWENTY-SIX

Elizabeth went inside at three to get ready for her date with John. Although she was excited about the prospect, as it got closer to five o'clock, she grew more and more nervous. "Why did I agree to this?" she mumbled as she washed her face. "I'm too old to date." Even as she said the words, she knew she was being ridiculous. She had older friends who'd found love late in life and had successfully married. "Now you're thinking about marriage?" she said to her image in the mirror. "It's just a date. Maybe he won't even like you. Maybe you won't like him."

She jumped when she heard a voice behind her. She whirled around with her toothbrush in her mouth. Mary stood there, frowning at her.

"He'll like you, and you'll like him. Don't ruin this by being negative."

Elizabeth removed her toothbrush, feeling silly for talking to herself. "I'm not being negative. Well, I'm not trying to be, anyway. I'm just so nervous."

"I know. But you can do this, Lizzie. You're such a wonderful person. Young, vital—with so much to give. If anyone should be nervous, it's John."

"What a nice thing to say." Elizabeth smiled at her younger sister. "Thank you. Sometimes I feel like an old woman. As if there's nothing left to give anyone." She put her toothbrush back in the holder. "I wish I could see myself differently."

Mary reached over and patted her shoulder. "You took good care of Mama, and it took a lot out of you. But she's gone, and you're still here. Time to start living."

"Why don't you put your money where your mouth is? Help me with my hair and makeup?"

Mary chuckled. "I can do that. Let me tell Martha I'll be inside a while. It's slow right now. I think most people go out early on Saturdays because they're also going to yard sales, and they want to get first crack at the bargains."

"I remember Mama saying the same thing."

"You go get dressed. I'll be right back."

While Mary went downstairs to coordinate with Martha, Elizabeth got the outfit she'd picked out of Mary's closet. A few minutes later she stood in front of the mirror, smiling. She'd liked it the first time she'd tried it on, and she liked it even more now. Since having her hair tinted, it seemed as if the silky gray-blue blouse was even more striking.

"Looks great," Mary said, coming into Elizabeth's bedroom. "Now sit down, and I'll add a few touches to make you look so good John's jaw will drop to the floor when he sees you."

Elizabeth giggled. "You make him sound like some cartoon character. I hope his jaw stays exactly where it's supposed to be."

Thirty minutes later, Elizabeth found herself staring into the mirror at someone she didn't recognize. "It's like I'm looking at someone who should be my daughter," she said breathlessly. "It's amazing what a little hair color and makeup can do."

"Oh, Lizzie, that's not it." Mary sat down next to her on the bench in front of her dressing table. "It's the look in your eyes and on your face. There's something there. Life. Animation. A spark. It's not your hairstyle or your makeup. It's all you."

Elizabeth laughed. "A spark? Really? What was I before. Sparkless?"

"That's not what I meant." Mary turned and looked away for a moment. When she turned her head around, Elizabeth was surprised to see tears in her eyes. "You looked like a woman who's spent several years caring for an elderly parent. Someone who wondered if her life was over. Someone who didn't want to leave the house." She pointed at the mirror. "The woman in that mirror believes a man finds her attractive. That she has an exciting life waiting to be lived."

Elizabeth's eyes flushed with tears too. "That was beautiful, Mary. But you're going to ruin my mascara."

The two women laughed. Mary got up and double-checked Elizabeth's hair. Then she lightly sprayed it so it would keep its gentle waves.

"Stay here a minute," she said. "I'll be right back."

Mary hurried out of the room while Elizabeth got to her feet. These pumps would probably make her feet hurt by the end of the night. She was trying to decide if she should take a coat when Mary came back into the room.

"Here. These will finish it off."

She handed Elizabeth some lovely silver dangly earrings. Elizabeth put them on and was thrilled to see how well they matched the blouse.

"You don't need a necklace with this blouse, but this tennis bracelet will look nice." Elizabeth stuck out her arm, and Mary fastened a lovely silver bracelet with small rhinestones around her wrist.

"Oh, Mary. It's gorgeous. Are you sure you want to lend it to me? You know how clumsy I can be. What if I lose it?"

"*Pfft.* You won't lose it. It's got a strong clasp."

She stood back and surveyed her older sister. "Oh, Lizzie. You look so beautiful."

"Thanks, Mary. Really. I don't know if I could go through with this without your help."

"You could, but you're welcome. That's what sisters are for, right?"

"Right." Elizabeth grabbed Mary's hand. "So tell me more about last night."

A slow smile spread across Mary's face. "Oh, Lizzie. He's so nice. I could talk to him so easily. We didn't even finish the movie. I think we could have talked all night. We're so alike. We believe so many of the same things."

"So you really like him?"

"I've always liked him, but last night I saw another side of him. I think… Well, I think, maybe, someday, we could be more than friends, but as I said, I'm just not ready for anything like that yet."

Elizabeth put her arms around her sister. "When it's time, you'll know it."

"I really haven't been sure I could ever think seriously about a man again. I hate that I've been so...injured. I detest women who spend their lives being victims."

"Oh, hon. That isn't you. Brian really hurt you. It takes time to heal from that. Only God can bring that kind of restoration."

Mary gently pulled away from Elizabeth's embrace. "I believe that. I also believe that sometimes God uses your sisters to help you become whole again."

Elizabeth dabbed at her wet eyes. "Yes," she whispered. "Yes, He does."

"I'm going to leave you alone now. I'm making you too emotional."

"Thanks, Mary. I guess I need to gather my courage a bit." She looked at herself in the mirror once again. "I still feel a little too old to be dating again."

"Well, obviously John disagrees. He sees something special in you."

Elizabeth turned around to smile at her. "You know what? You're right. Maybe this old mare ain't what she used to be, but obviously she's still got a little something going on."

Mary laughed. "Yes, she does. You'll be fine, Lizzie. Just be yourself." Mary left the room, closing the door behind her.

Elizabeth sat down in front of her dressing table again. Her stomach fluttered with excitement...and nervousness. What Mary said was true. She sighed deeply and stared at her reflection. "You can do this, Lizzie," she said softly. "If things don't work out with John, it's okay. You'll meet someone else. If you'll just take the chance, you could still have a life. You have to try. Please. Be brave." Suddenly the words of one of her favorite

Bible teachers came back to her. *"Sometimes you'll feel fear,"* she'd said, *"but don't back down. Learn to do it afraid."*

Although Elizabeth didn't feel any different, she stood up, found her purse, and went out to the porch to wait for John to arrive. She felt as if she were holding on to her courage with both hands, as hard as she could, determined not to let go.

CHAPTER TWENTY-SEVEN

After Elizabeth left, Mary grabbed her purse, got the keys to Elizabeth's car, and snuck out without telling Martha where she was going. She didn't want to explain ahead of time, but she was determined to set things right. Sharing her plan with her sisters might make her change her mind. This was something she needed to do—no matter how frightened she was.

She got into the car, said a prayer, and headed to town.

As silly as it sounded, in Elizabeth's mind she had somehow expected John to wear his uniform on their date. She realized that she'd been so worried about how *she* looked she'd never considered that he would wear civilian clothes when he was off duty. Although she held a menu in front of her, she couldn't stop looking at him. He was dressed in a light-blue polo shirt and dark-blue slacks. The shirt brought out his blue eyes and black hair. He was even more handsome out of uniform. Elizabeth kept wondering why someone like him would be interested in her. He could get any woman he wanted. Why wasn't he married? Why wasn't he dating someone else? Why had he asked her out? She kept trying to push the questions away, but they would sneak back in without her even realizing it.

"Have you decided?" he asked her with a smile.

She quickly lowered her eyes to the menu. Even though she hadn't actually looked at it, she'd eaten here enough to know what she wanted. "I think I'll go with the pecan-crusted tilapia. It's delicious."

He nodded. "It is good. Hard to pick, but I feel like having roast beef. Never had a bad meal here."

Elizabeth had just closed the menu and put it on the table when the waitress walked up. They gave her their orders, and she took the menus away.

"So, what did you think of the play?" John asked.

Elizabeth smiled. "I loved it. I haven't been to the theater for years. I forgot how much I enjoy it."

"May I ask why you stayed away for so long?"

"Taking care of elderly parents. My mother died a few months ago."

"Your sisters didn't help you?"

"They lived in other states. After Mama passed away, they came here to live. We decided to reopen the secondhand store my grandmother started years ago."

"You've been through a lot, Elizabeth," he said. "It must have been hard."

"It really wasn't that bad. When you love someone, caring for them is…a blessing. I adored my mother, and I miss her every day."

John nodded. "My wife was sick for a long time. I kept working until...I couldn't. Being there for her at the end was something I wanted to do more than anything else in the world."

"I—I had no idea you'd been married."

He smiled. "It was a long time ago. Carol's been gone almost fifteen years now. Funny how grief changes, but it doesn't ever go away."

"I know exactly what you mean," Elizabeth said. "Some people don't understand that."

"No, they don't."

"Do you have any children, John?"

This time his smile had no hint of sadness. "Yes, I do. My son, Jonathan, is in college, and Tina is still in high school."

"And in all these years, you never married again?"

He shook his head. "I felt I needed to concentrate on the kids. I've dated some, but I've never found anyone I felt was the right person for me." He chuckled. "Being perfectly honest, I'm not sure I even know what that means anymore."

"I understand completely. I was engaged once, but now..." Elizabeth clasped her hands in front of her. "I have no idea what I want. Or if I'll ever find the right person. I haven't thought about it for years."

John picked up his glass and held it out. "Well, here's to navigating the dangerous waters of dating."

Elizabeth laughed and picked up her water glass, touching it lightly against his. They each took a sip and put their glasses down. "I'm having such a good time, John. Thanks for asking me."

"I'm having a great time too. I hope we can do this again."

"I do too."

Elizabeth was surprised by how relaxed she felt. With John, she didn't feel as if she was on a date. Instead, she was sharing an enjoyable evening with a friend. She was so grateful she'd decided to say yes to his invitation. Since they'd both been honest about their past, the pressure had been lessened.

"I wish I had some news about your break-in," he said, "but so far we haven't gotten a lead."

Elizabeth's heart sank. She should have contacted him right away after Eleanor Wallace had confessed to them. She'd been so distracted by other things, she'd totally forgotten. "Oh, John, I'm so sorry. You're going to think I'm the biggest ditz in the world."

The waitress came by at that moment to freshen their coffee. When she left he smiled at her.

"I doubt I'm going to think anything like that, but tell me why you think I should."

She took a deep breath. "Because there wasn't a break-in. Well, I mean, I guess there was, but..."

He frowned at her. "Either there was or there wasn't, Elizabeth. It has to be one way or the other."

"I know, I know. Let me think how to explain." She cleared her throat and began again. "The woman who...broke into our barn was a distraught mother, looking for something for her sick child."

John looked confused. "Wouldn't it have been better to shop when you were open?"

Even though the conversation was serious, Elizabeth couldn't hold back a nervous giggle. "No, that's not what I mean." She shook her head. "I'm sorry. For some reason, I'm being obtuse." She looked at him directly. "Warren Smucker had a painting in his home. He promised his housekeeper, Eleanor Wallace, that when he died, her daughter, Kelly, could have it. It's a copy of a famous painting, but it's not valuable. It's just something Kelly loved. When he died, Anita gave it to us to sell. Then, when she thought it might be worth a great deal of money, she took it back without telling us. We thought it had been stolen and that we would be liable for it."

"I'm sorry," John said in a low voice, "but I don't understand what this has to do with anything."

"You will when I finish."

He nodded at her to continue.

"Well, anyway, Eleanor found out we had the painting and came when we were open, looking for it. When we told her we didn't have it, she thought we were lying…"

"So she broke into your barn looking for it."

Elizabeth smiled triumphantly. "Yes, that's it."

"That's still against the law. Everyone has a reason for breaking into someone else's property. That doesn't make it legal."

"Well, no. It doesn't. But we don't want to press charges. You see, her daughter, Kelly, has leukemia. Eleanor was just distraught. She was trying to get the painting for Kelly so it would make her happy."

"And you didn't think to tell me this? You or your sisters?"

"It's stupid. We've just been so distracted." She suddenly remembered the feeling the other night that she'd forgotten something. Now she knew what it was. "I'm so sorry. I hope you can find it in your heart to forgive me. Somewhere inside I knew I needed to let you know about Eleanor, but with everything else going on, it got pushed out of my mind."

Thankfully, he smiled. "I'm glad you weren't really robbed. But promise me the next time something like this happens you'll let me know."

Relieved that he wasn't angry, Elizabeth chuckled. "I promise, but hopefully nothing like this will ever happen again. Most thieves don't pick secondhand shops as places to target. We don't usually have the kinds of items they're looking for."

"Good." He frowned. "So what happened with the picture?"

"Anita Smucker gave it to Eleanor, and now Kelly has the painting."

"So it turned out well. I'm glad."

"Me too."

The waitress brought their food, so they turned their attention to dinner. When they finished eating, they talked for a while and then went outside and got into John's car. They'd just turned onto the street outside the restaurant when John's cell phone rang. He answered it and seemed concerned about what he was hearing. When he hung up he turned to look at her.

"I'm really sorry, but we just got a call from Bird-in-Hand, and I'm the closest. Everyone else is busy somewhere else. Do you mind? It's not a violent crime. If you'd rather, I can take you home first."

"I don't mind at all. Please do what you need to do."

Although stopping by a crime scene hadn't been on their agenda, Elizabeth found it interesting. Besides, since she knew most of the people in Bird-in-Hand, she was concerned that one of her neighbors might be in trouble.

John turned down a couple of streets and drove through a well-known neighborhood. Elizabeth stayed silent until he parked in front of a house she was very familiar with. Uriah Barnhart's.

"Can you tell me why we're here?"

"Do you know Mr. Barnhart?"

Elizabeth nodded.

"He called the station to say he'd been robbed. Someone stole something valuable. I believe he said it was a Civil War sword."

Elizabeth just looked at him, not knowing what to say.

"Just stay here. I'll be right back."

As she watched him walk toward the house, all she could think about was Mary saying they should break into Uriah's house and steal the sword. Had she actually done it?

CHAPTER TWENTY-EIGHT

Elizabeth sat in the car for a few minutes, thinking. Finally she took her cell phone out of her purse and called home. The phone rang a few times before Martha answered. Keeping an eye on Uriah's front door, Elizabeth asked her if Mary was there.

"Well, no," she said. "I heard her leave a couple of hours ago. She didn't tell me where she was going, and I haven't seen her since. Why? Is she in some kind of trouble?"

"Why would you ask that?" Elizabeth said.

"Oh, I don't know. Maybe it's because you're calling while you're on a date, and you sound upset. What's going on?"

"I honestly don't know. I'm sitting outside of Uriah's house. He called the police, and John responded. Someone took his sword."

Martha was silent, making it clear that her mind had gone exactly where Elizabeth's was.

"Surely you don't think…," Martha said finally.

"I don't know what to think. Mary's not a thief, but you know how impulsive she can be. She acts without thinking."

"I know, Lizzie, but she's always been a very honest person."

Elizabeth sighed. "I hope so."

"Is John with you now?"

"He's inside with Uriah. Martha, we messed up. We didn't call him after we found out about Eleanor. He was still looking for our *burglar*."

"Nonsense," she said. "I called the police station and left the information with the woman who answered the phone."

"Really? Well, it never got to John. I don't suppose you remember the name of the person you talked to."

"Of course I do. It was Rose."

"And you told her to pass the information on to John?"

"Of course I did." She sighed. "I don't know what happened, Lizzie. But the fault isn't ours. You need to tell him to check with this Rose person."

"Absolutely. Thanks, Martha. I should have known you'd do the responsible thing. Hey, John's coming out. Can I call you back?"

"Sure. I'll be here."

"Okay." Elizabeth groaned when she saw Uriah on John's heels. The last thing she wanted to do was to talk to him. As they approached, she rolled down her window. The expression on John's face stopped her short.

"Elizabeth," John said as he came up to the window, "Mr. Barnhart seems to think you had something to do with the disappearance of his sword."

Elizabeth shook her head. "That's not true. How would I know what happened to it?"

"Because you stole it!" Uriah yelled. "I know you have it." He turned his attention to John. "Arrest her. Arrest her right now and tell her to return my property." His voice was so loud that people in the neighborhood came out on their porches to see what was going on. "She's a thief, I tell you. Throw her in jail, but first ask her what she did with it!"

John leaned down until his face was level with hers. "I'm so sorry about this, Elizabeth. He says the sword was stolen a couple of hours ago. I told him we were at the play during that time, but he won't believe me."

Elizabeth took a deep breath, trying to calm her nerves. "Mr. Barnhart, I truly didn't take your sword." She pointed at John. "Do you still have the ticket stubs from the play?"

He snapped his fingers. "Of course. I should have thought of that." He reached into the pocket of his slacks and pulled out the stubs. "See?" he said, showing them to Uriah. "The play started at six o'clock. It lasted two hours. Then we went to dinner." He pulled out his billfold and took out the restaurant receipt. "The time is stamped on this. I'm telling you that Elizabeth was with me since five o'clock. I can assure you she didn't take your sword. It's not possible."

Uriah looked like someone had slapped him in the face. "I still think you're involved somehow," he blustered. He pointed at John. "You need to look into this. Check out her sisters. I'll bet one of them did it. They've been trying to get me to give them back this sword ever since I bought it from them." A look of triumph washed over his face.

John sighed and looked at her. "I take it this is one of the things that belonged to Anita Smucker?"

Elizabeth nodded. "She was particularly upset about the sword, but she doesn't know if it's valuable. Neither do we. I've been doing some research and haven't found anything that would lead us to believe this is what Anita's been looking for."

She nodded toward Uriah. "I'm sorry the sword's gone, Mr. Barnhart, but I had nothing to do with its disappearance, and I'm certain Anita didn't either. As I just said, there's no evidence the sword is worth more than a few hundred dollars."

"Anita Smucker wants that sword because of her great-great-grandfather. Not because it's worth a lot of money." He glared at John. "You need to go check out that woman's house. I'll bet you'll find it."

"First you're sure Elizabeth broke into your house and stole something. Now you think it's Anita Smucker?" John shook his head. "You haven't given me anything that I'd call probable cause. I'll file a report, and we'll do everything we can to find your sword, but I'm not going to bother the Classen sisters or Miss Smucker without evidence."

Uriah's face wrinkled into a sneer, and Elizabeth was certain steam would shoot out of his ears at any moment. He'd turned and started to stomp back toward his house when John called him back. Convinced he would ignore John, she was surprised when he walked back toward the car.

"Mr. Barnhart," John said when he got closer, "I understand you hardly ever leave your home. Did you go anywhere this evening?"

"Not that it's any of your business, but I had to pick up my medicine. My pharmacy has started charging for deliveries. It's highway robbery, and I'm not going to pay it."

"Who else knew you were going to the pharmacy?"

"No one!" he insisted. "I'm not in the habit of telling people my business."

"Mr. Barnhart, this is important," Elizabeth said. "Please think about it."

"Why? So you can blame someone else for what you and your sisters did? No, thank you." With that, he turned around and headed for his front door. Once inside, he slammed it behind him.

"That was a good question," Elizabeth said.

"I suspect someone found out he wouldn't be home. That person will likely be our thief."

"That makes sense."

John gestured toward the house. "I need to go inside, take some pictures, ask questions..."

"I understand. I'll call my sisters and ask one of them to pick me up. You don't have to worry about me."

Elizabeth had just finished speaking when a police car pulled up behind them.

"Hold on. We may be saved. Let me talk to these guys." John walked over to the squad car and spoke to the officers inside. Then he came back to the car and got inside. "They're going to take it from here." He started the car. "I know it's late, but how about dessert?"

"The sidewalks are rolled up early in Bird-in-Hand. Just where do you suggest we go?"

John grinned. "I understand you know someone who's a fabulous baker."

"Are you actually inviting yourself over?"

John feigned a look of innocence. "Would I do that?"

Elizabeth giggled. "It's a great idea. Let me call Martha real quick and warn her." She dialed the house and asked

Martha if it was okay for her to bring John to the house for dessert.

"Are you serious?" Martha asked. "I'd love it. In fact, I just took an Italian cream cake out of the oven."

"My favorite?" Elizabeth asked.

"Yes, Lizzie. I made it for you. To celebrate your decision to get out and live your life." Martha chuckled. "And no, I won't say that in front of John. You're safe."

Elizabeth laughed, grateful her sister had made it clear she wasn't going to say something embarrassing in front of John. "Okay. We're on our way."

"Good. You can bring me up to date on Uriah."

"I will. I hope Mary will be back by the time we get there."

"I hope so too. See you soon."

Elizabeth hung up and smiled at John. "You're in for a treat. Martha just made my favorite dessert. Italian cream cake. Have you ever had any?"

He shook his head. "Can't say I have, but it sounds great."

"It is. Thankfully, Martha doesn't make it a lot. Too many calories."

He laughed. "Not something you need to worry about. By the way, is it okay if I tell you how lovely you look tonight?"

Elizabeth looked away, her heart beating so hard she wondered if John could hear it. "Of course you can."

"I noticed how beautiful you were the first time I met you. But when you started to talk... Well, I knew you were someone special. Tonight has proven me right."

Elizabeth felt her face grow hot. "Thank you. I don't know what to say."

"You don't have to say anything except that you'll go out with me again."

She looked into his eyes. "Yes. I'd like that."

He smiled and put the car into gear.

As they drove toward Elizabeth's house, she wanted to revel in the warmth of John's words, but worry about Mary kept crowding them out.

CHAPTER TWENTY-NINE

This just might be the best thing I've ever tasted," John said as he took a bite of his second helping of cake. "Where did you get the recipe?"

"It's our mother's," Martha said. "People used to order cakes from her for special occasions. She got the recipe from an old friend. It's not the easiest cake to make, but the effort is worth it."

"I love coconut cream pie, but this is even better." He scooped up another bite of the coconut cake with cream cheese frosting and pecans. "This could get addictive. I understand why you don't make it very often." He made quick work of his next bite. "Did you bake this for a special occasion?" He looked at Elizabeth. "It's not your birthday or anything, is it?"

"No, it's not her birthday," Martha said quickly. "I just wanted to bless her. She's been working so hard, and we've been under so much pressure, I felt she needed something to lift her spirits."

"Well, I hope it worked, Elizabeth. I know it certainly made me feel better."

"I'm glad you like it so much," Martha said, smiling.

John put his fork down. "So what's going on with the search for that special item Anita is trying to find?"

"Before we answer that," Elizabeth said, "I need to tell you that Martha did call your office to tell them we didn't need you to continue our case."

"You did?" John asked, looking at Martha. "Who did you talk to?"

"Someone named Rose, who said she'd give you the message."

John sighed. "That explains it. Rose is a woman who stops by frequently to tell us someone has stolen her parakeet." He shook his head. "Rose doesn't have a parakeet."

"Why would she answer the phone?" Martha asked.

"I suspect our administrative assistant, Donna, was away from her desk for a moment."

"But she sounded so competent."

John nodded. "She can. Until she tells you about the aliens who are roaming the streets looking for parakeets. She's a sweet woman who is just a little confused."

"A *little* confused?" Elizabeth asked.

"Well, maybe a lot confused. I'm sorry about that, Martha," he said. "Thanks for calling to let us know."

"You're welcome. I hope Eleanor won't get in any trouble."

"Not from me. If you say nothing was stolen, and you don't want to press charges over the break-in, it's no skin off my nose. I'll just close the case."

"Thank you," Mary said. "I wouldn't want to add anything else to the load Eleanor is already carrying."

"Maybe we can help some," John said. "We have a fund for citizens in need, including those who have sick kids. If she lost her job and her child is ill, I'm sure we can do something."

"Oh, John, that would be fantastic," Elizabeth said.

"Yes, it would." Martha stood and got a plastic food storage container. "Just for that, I'm sending some of this cake home with you."

John's wide smile made it clear he was thrilled. "Maybe Elizabeth doesn't want to share her special blessing."

Martha grinned at her sister. "How about it, Lizzie? Do you mind sharing your cake?"

"Oh please. Getting it out of the house is the only way to ensure I won't eat the whole thing."

"Well, I guess I can take some just to help you," John said.

"I really appreciate the sacrifice." Elizabeth laughed. Even with Uriah's meltdown and her concern about Mary, this night had turned out better than she'd ever expected. She was just about to tease John a little more when she heard a car pull up outside. She looked at Martha, who locked eyes with her. They were quiet as they heard the car door open and close. A few seconds later the door swung open, and Mary walked in.

"Well, what have we here?" she asked, a big smile on her face. "Italian cream cake? Awesome! Can I have a piece?"

"Of course." Martha got a plate and cut a piece for Mary.

Mary sat down at the table. "So did you two have a good time?" she asked, directing her question to John and Elizabeth.

"It was very enjoyable," John said. "The play was great and dinner was delicious, but the company was the best part."

Mary winked at Elizabeth. "Great. I'm so happy to hear it."

She dug into her cake as if she hadn't eaten in days. Elizabeth was confused by her demeanor. If she'd stolen the sword, walking into the house and finding a police officer should have unnerved her. On the contrary, Mary looked almost jubilant.

"You said something about some kind of riddle that Warren Smucker left behind," John said. "Would you mind if I looked at it?"

"Of course not." Elizabeth got up and got the riddle out of the drawer. She handed it to John and then grabbed the coffeepot. "Anyone want more?" she asked. Martha declined, but John nodded. She brought the pot over and filled his cup.

"I'd love some, Sis," Mary said.

Elizabeth brought Mary a cup of coffee. If her sister was feeling guilty, she was doing an extraordinary job of hiding it.

Elizabeth put the pot back on the coffee maker and slid into her chair. John was muttering to himself as he read the riddle.

"Boy," he said finally, "this doesn't make much sense. Have you figured out anything about it?"

Elizabeth told him everything they'd come up with so far.

"A thunderbird? Lightning bolts? You think this points to the sword?"

"It was the only thing that made sense," Martha said.

John frowned. "I'm not an expert on the Civil War, but I've seen a few old swords. Usually the bird is an eagle, and what he holds in his talons are arrows."

"We wondered about that," Mary said. "Elizabeth, show him your pictures."

Elizabeth got her phone from her purse, brought up the pictures, and handed the phone to John.

He scrolled through several of them. "Yeah, I think you're looking at an eagle with arrows. I'm not saying there aren't swords out there with thunderbirds and lightning bolts, but I don't think this is one of them."

"I kind of hate to hear that," Elizabeth said. "The sword is the only thing we've researched so far that comes close to matching the riddle. Supposedly, it belonged to Stonewall Jackson. That would make it very valuable if we could just prove it."

"Hey!" Mary said suddenly. "I just thought of something. We know that Warren was pretty addlebrained right before he died…"

"Mary!" Martha said. "That's not appropriate."

Mary's smile vanished. "I'm sorry. I'm not trying to be disrespectful. I just meant that he was confused. We keep wondering if the entire riddle is nonsense because…because of his condition." She looked at Martha for approval and seemed to find it. "You know, maybe we're wrong to throw out the baby with the bathwater, so to speak. What if some of his descriptions are just off? You see what I mean? Maybe to him the eagle was a thunderbird and the arrows were lightning bolts."

"Certainly," Elizabeth said. "The riddle could actually be right, but when Warren wrote it, he confused certain aspects of it. Maybe thinking about it that way will finally help us solve it."

"Sounds great," Martha said sarcastically. "So now all we have to do is interpret the riddle with the wrong answers?"

"You're right," Mary said. "Instead of helping us, it might actually make it harder to solve."

"I guess it depends on how addlebrained *we* are," Elizabeth said.

Martha and Mary both laughed.

John nodded at Mary. "Still, I think what you said makes some sense. Maybe if you can see the riddle through Warren's eyes, it will help. You see an eagle, he sees a thunderbird. You see arrows, he sees lightning bolts. It might be the only way to interpret this thing."

"Maybe so," Elizabeth said. "I guess we should start using the references in the riddle a little more...loosely."

John gazed at the words on the paper again. "I wish I could help, but I'm afraid I don't have a clue. Swords, cousins, thunderbirds... It's confusing." He took his cell phone out of his pocket and took a quick picture of the riddle. "I'll keep thinking about it though. Maybe I can dig up something that will bring you closer to an answer."

"Thanks, John," Martha said. "At this point, we can use all the support we can get. We really need to prove the sword belonged to Jackson, or find reason to believe it's another item. If we can prove the sword's authenticity, I believe we've found the treasure. Not that it will help Anita."

John took another sip of coffee and yawned. "Sorry. Getting a little late for me, and I have an early morning. I certainly appreciate the hospitality." He smiled at Elizabeth. "Walk me to my car?"

"Of course." Elizabeth stood up and waited for him to join her at the door. "I hope to see you both again soon," he said to Martha and Mary.

"I'm sure we will," Mary said, looking back and forth between him and Elizabeth, a smile on her face.

John opened the door, and Elizabeth walked out onto the porch. She waited for him, and they walked to his car together.

"What will happen next with Uriah?" she asked him when he leaned against the driver's door.

"Well, hopefully we'll find a clue at the scene. We'll also interview the neighbors to see if anyone noticed something amiss. You know, someone in or near Uriah's house who shouldn't be there. Or even someone who should."

"Do you suspect anyone in particular?"

"No, but we need to check out delivery people, anyone who could have found out about the sword. Many times this line of questioning leads us to our suspects. We'll check with the neighbors. Someone might have seen something important. People are a lot more observant than you might think."

"Or nosier?"

His warm laughter made Elizabeth feel good. She was impressed with his kindness and compassion. But she also respected him because of the choice he'd made to serve the public.

"I really did have a great time," he said when she turned to look at him.

"I did too." Even though she'd been pretty relaxed the entire evening, except during Uriah's outburst, at that moment she felt shy and awkward.

"How about next week?" he asked. "Friday night?"

Elizabeth nodded. "I'd like that."

"Good. I'll call you."

Elizabeth said goodbye and walked back to the porch. She watched him as he drove away. Tonight had stirred up feelings she hadn't had in many years, but she knew she needed to find out something soon, before this went much further. Was John a man of faith?

CHAPTER THIRTY

When Elizabeth opened the door, Martha and Mary were waiting for her, still sitting at the table.

Mary frowned at her. "Martha says you two want to talk to me. Has something happened?"

Elizabeth sighed and sat down across from her. "As a matter of fact, it has. Tonight, after dinner, John had to take a call in Bird-in-Hand. It was a theft. At Uriah Barnhart's."

Mary's mouth dropped open, and her eyes widened. "You're kidding. The sword? Did someone take the sword?"

"Yes, Mary," Elizabeth said. "Someone took the sword."

Mary's eyes narrowed. "What are you saying? Surely you don't think I did it."

"We have to wonder," Martha said. "You threatened to break in and steal it."

"I did not," Mary said emphatically. "I said it was an idea. I never said I really wanted to take that sword."

"So you promise us you didn't take it?" Martha asked.

Mary sighed. "Of course I do. How could you possibly suspect me?"

Elizabeth crossed her arms and leaned back in her chair. "Well, you acted like stealing the sword might be a good idea. Then you disappeared without telling us where you were going. And then the sword was stolen."

"So you're conclusion is that I'm a thief?"

"Don't put this on us," Martha said sternly. "You do tend to act before you think sometimes."

"I'm not a teenager anymore. Perhaps you've noticed? You keep judging me by the person I was when I was young. It's really not fair."

"You might be right," Elizabeth said. "But even though your heart's in the right place, you can still be impulsive."

"Not always. Sometimes I'm just too careful."

"What do you mean?" Elizabeth asked.

"Like when it comes to dating."

Martha pointed at her. "Just where were you tonight, Mary?"

"Well, I certainly wasn't breaking into Uriah Barnhart's house," she said sarcastically. "I was…" Her lips quivered into a small smile. "I was at Bill's house. I went there to tell him that, if he was still interested, I think I'm ready to go out on a real date with him."

Elizabeth was silent for a moment as the reality of Mary's words sunk in. Martha must have had the same reaction, because she just stared at Mary for several seconds with her mouth open.

"Mary…," Elizabeth finally choked out. "Don't you think that's…that's…"

Martha finished her sentence. "A little forward?"

Mary frowned. "How is that forward? What's wrong with being open and honest? If I don't tell him, how's he gonna know?"

Elizabeth grinned. Mary had a point. "I admire your courage," she said.

"Sorry to disappoint you about the sword," Mary said, "but tonight Uriah Barnhart was the last thing on my mind."

"We're sorry," Elizabeth said. "This thing with Anita has us both on pins and needles. I know you're not a thief. I just went crazy, I guess."

"It's okay. Frankly, I would have suspected me too."

Martha leaned forward, searching Mary's face. "So tell us about Bill. What did you say? What did he say?"

Mary ran her fingers through her blond hair. "Well, when he answered the door he looked surprised, but he invited me in. He has the cutest house. An old craftsman home. He's completely remodeled it. Wood beams, built-in bookcases—"

"Mary!" Martha exclaimed. "We don't want to hear about his house. What did you tell him?"

Mary took a deep breath and let it out slowly. "Well, I told him that I'd been hurt badly by Brian. That after what I'd been through, I've been afraid of having feelings for anyone else. But…that for the first time since Brian left me, I think I'm ready to take a chance, or at least explore the possibilities. I told Bill how much I like him—what a good man I think he is. Then I told him if he was still interested, I'd like to go out with him."

Elizabeth realized they sounded like love struck teenagers, but she didn't care. "And what did he say?" she asked.

"He said he certainly was still interested, and then he asked me out Friday night."

Martha clapped her hands together. "That's wonderful."

"John asked me out Friday night too," Elizabeth said slowly.

Martha frowned at her. "So? Surely you don't think I can't take care of myself without you two."

"It's not that, Sis," she said. "I don't like the idea of you sitting here alone."

Martha burst out laughing. "Seriously? Has it ever occurred to you two that a night by myself might sound fantastic? I can eat what I want, I'll finally have control of the remote…" She grinned at them. "I love you both, but after Chuck died and the kids moved out, I got used to being alone. There are a lot of things I like about it. I wouldn't want to go back to living by myself, but having some quiet time would be really nice."

"Okay," Elizabeth said. "If you're sure."

"Oh, I'm sure." She smiled. "I'm so thrilled for you both. The Classen girls are going out. I'm truly happy about it."

"I am too," Mary said. "It almost feels like part of me is coming to life again. I know that sounds silly, but—"

"No, it doesn't sound silly at all," Elizabeth said. "I understand completely."

Martha picked up the dirty dishes on the table and carried them to the sink. "You two are gonna make me cry if you keep it up."

"I still think you'll find someone again someday, Martha," Mary said.

She shrugged. "Maybe, but I'm really not interested, and I'm not just saying that. I still feel that Chuck is part of me. When I get to heaven I don't want some other guy following me around. It would just irritate me."

Mary and Elizabeth laughed.

Martha loaded the dirty dishes in the dishwasher, added dishwashing powder, and turned it on. "Now I think we'd all better get to bed. Church comes early in the morning."

"What about the sword?" Mary asked. "Who do you think took it?"

"There's only one person I can think of," Martha said. "Anita Smucker."

Elizabeth yawned, suddenly aware of how tired she was. "I hope you're wrong," she said. "But the same thought crossed my mind."

"Does John think she might be involved?"

"I don't know," Elizabeth said. "The only thing he mentioned was that Uriah hadn't given him good enough reasons for probable cause to search her house. I think he's focused on someone else who might have known Uriah would be gone earlier this evening."

Martha was silent for a moment. "I wonder if we should say something to Anita about the sword."

"I'm not sure." Elizabeth turned Martha's suggestion over in her mind. "I don't want her to think we suspect her. But I also don't want to tip her off if she did take it."

"But how would Anita know when Uriah was going to be gone?" Mary asked.

"That's true. And it's probably one reason John is looking in another direction. He—"

"What's the matter, Elizabeth?" Mary asked. "You look like you've seen a ghost."

"Not a ghost," she said. "But I may have seen a thief. Or something a thief left behind." She glanced at the clock. A little after nine o'clock. "I hope Uriah doesn't go to bed early." She reached for her purse and removed her cell phone.

"What are you talking about?" Martha asked. "Why would you talk to that old goat after he accused you of stealing a rusty old sword?"

"Elizabeth was accused too?" Mary responded, surprise in her voice.

"Actually, he mentioned all of us," Elizabeth said. She opened her purse again and fumbled around until she found the card John had given her the night of the break-in. She dialed the number. John answered almost immediately.

"Are you already missing me?" he asked. "I'm not even home yet."

"Funny. I just remembered something that might be important." She told him what she'd noticed at Uriah's.

"Exactly what I was looking for," he said. "We need to find out if he knew when Uriah would be gone, but if he did, I think we've got our thief. Thanks, Elizabeth. I'm going to Uriah's now to question him. I'll let you know tomorrow what I find out."

"Thanks, John." She hung up the phone and grinned at her sisters. "We'll find out tomorrow if we just solved a crime."

"If *you* solved a crime," Martha said. "We just sat here and did nothing."

"You made me think. With a little luck, we'll soon know exactly what happened to the sword."

CHAPTER THIRTY-ONE

After church, the sisters drove to Lancaster to meet John for lunch at a local pizza restaurant. Capricio's Italian Grill and Kitchen was a small, unassuming restaurant tucked into a storefront, but the pizza was amazing. Elizabeth had been there several times and had taken Martha and Mary once since they'd moved back to Bird-in-Hand.

"Hope this is okay," John said when they arrived. "It's not fancy, but it's one of my favorite restaurants. If you don't like pizza, they have a lot of other Italian dishes."

"We love Capricio's," Elizabeth said. "This was a great choice."

Elizabeth decided to go with the Italian salad while Martha and Mary chose pizza. John ordered a calzone that looked delicious.

After they got their food, Elizabeth asked John why he wanted to talk to them.

"First of all, I enjoy your company. But secondly, I knew you'd want to know what I found out after I left your house last night."

"You have our attention," Martha said. "We've been on pins and needles all morning."

John's eyes sparkled with humor. "I drove over to Mr. Barnhart's and asked him a couple of questions. He does have a phone, by the way. I have the number. He doesn't like to hand it out to many people, but I told him I was giving it to you. I explained to him that making you drive all the way over to his house when you've been trying to help him is bad manners. I think he felt a little guilty about that."

"I've never known him to feel guilty about anything," Elizabeth said with a smile. "So you're already way ahead of us."

"I asked him if he'd told anyone he wasn't going to be home during the time he was going to the pharmacy. At first he said no. But after thinking about it for a while, he realized he'd mentioned it to one person. At the time he was complaining about his pharmacy starting to charge for delivery."

"Let me guess," Elizabeth said. "He complained to the guy who delivers milk."

John pointed at her. "Exactly. No one thinks about the milkman. He's just someone in the background. Someone you don't pay attention to."

"Well, we certainly pay attention to the person who delivers our milk." Elizabeth smiled to herself at the thought of Phoebe Fischer. "But I know what you mean."

She thought she detected a note of admiration in John's voice when he said, "You figured out who the thief was. Tell your sisters how you did it."

"I remembered leaving Uriah's house and almost tripping over two full bottles of milk on the front porch. That meant the delivery man had been there while we were talking about the sword and how valuable it might be. The door was open. The delivery man could have easily heard our conversation through the screen door."

John nodded. "I asked Mr. Barnhart about that, and he came to the same conclusion you did. Then when he realized he'd complained to the same guy about having to pick up his medicines, he put two and two together. Obviously, while Uriah was gone, the delivery guy went inside and grabbed the sword."

"How did he get in?" Mary asked. "Did he break the door?"

John shook his head. "Uriah keeps a key under the mat on the front porch. Don't know how the thief knew. Uriah could have mentioned it, or the guy just looked around and found it on his own. After he took the sword he relocked the door. That's why Mr. Barnhart didn't notice it was gone right away."

"Tell me you found the sword," Elizabeth said.

John smiled. "We found the sword."

"Will you give it back to Uriah?" Martha asked.

"After we release it. Right now it's evidence."

"At least now you know I didn't take it," Mary said.

John frowned. "Why would anyone think you took it?"

Mary laughed. "Ask my sisters."

Elizabeth sighed. "Anita promised a thousand dollars to anyone who could get the sword back. Mary made a joke about that, so when we found out it was stolen and that Mary had gone out…"

John's hearty laugh only made Elizabeth feel worse. Why had she and Martha jumped to such a silly conclusion? She was determined to show her sister more trust in the future. Frankly, Mary was right. Sometimes Elizabeth still saw her as the irresponsible teenager she used to be. Mary deserved better. And she probably needed it.

"Believe me," Martha said, "we've apologized more than once. Mary has been gracious enough to forgive us. This situation with Anita has made us all a little nuts."

Elizabeth had an awful thought. "John, is there any chance Anita paid this guy to steal the sword?"

He shook his head. "The thought occurred to me too, but he doesn't know Anita."

"I thought everyone in town knows who the Smuckers are."

"He knew the Smucker name, of course. It's famous in these parts. But he didn't know Anita or anything about her particular line of the family," he replied. "He lives over in Strasburg. Guess he doesn't spend much time here unless he's working." He nodded at Elizabeth. "Have you made a final decision about the sword's value?"

Elizabeth shook her head and sighed. "I've taken my research about as far as I can. The next step is to contact an expert in Civil War history. I can recommend some to Anita, but she'll have to pay for it. Their fees are pretty steep."

"The reason I ask is because I know a guy who might be able to help you. I don't know why I didn't think of him last night. I've known him a long time. He's a collector of Civil War stuff, and very knowledgeable about that period of history. I hope you don't mind, but I sent him some pictures."

"I don't mind at all," Elizabeth said. "Any assistance we can get is great, but I already talked to an antique dealer who specializes in Civil War memorabilia, and he couldn't help me."

"Well, my guy might not give us any information either, but I guess it doesn't hurt to ask." After taking a bite of his calzone, he asked, "So if the sword turns out to be Jackson's and is worth a lot of money, what happens next? I mean, it's not in Anita's possession. Will you tell Uriah what you find out?"

"I have to. I promised I'd share anything important."

"Even so, I don't think he'd sell it," Martha said. "The rumor is he has lots of money squirreled away. If so, he doesn't need to get rid of it. To be honest, I think he likes knowing he has something Anita wants."

"That seems cruel," Mary said. "If Anita doesn't find what her father left her, she'll have to sell her home. She'll be broke. If the sword really is valuable, how could Uriah live with himself knowing she was ruined by...a mistake?"

"I'm sorry to say it," Elizabeth said with a sigh, "but I doubt he'll care. I haven't seen much compassion in him."

"I think he's lonely," Mary said.

"That's his own fault," Elizabeth said. "He doesn't have to be alone. According to Mama, people have reached out to him time after time. He chooses to stay holed up in that creepy old house. She was one of the only people he'd talk to."

"Any idea why he lives like that?" John asked.

Elizabeth shook her head. "I have no idea. He used to be a member of our church. Started attending not long after Mary and Martha moved away. He quit going about nine years ago, I think. Not long after he retired."

"I've been curious about Uriah too," Martha said. "I asked Ruth about him today. Seems he fell in love when he was in his twenties. With a woman who married someone else."

"That's what made him so cranky?" Mary asked. "Shouldn't he have gotten over that by now?"

"No, there's more. Ruth said he and this woman, Doris, got together again after her divorce. Doris had a teenage grandson named Brandon who lived with her. Uriah and Brandon became very close. To Uriah, he was the son he'd never had. Doris and Uriah planned to get married."

"And she married someone else again?" Mary guessed.

Martha shook her head. "Worse. Doris and Brandon went to a family reunion in Nebraska a couple of weeks before the wedding. They asked Uriah to come with them. They wanted to introduce him to their family, but he was too busy with work and decided to stay here. On the way to the reunion, the driver of a semi-truck fell asleep and crossed over the median on the highway. He slammed right into their car. They were both killed."

Elizabeth's eyes filled with tears. Frankly, it was hard to see Uriah as a man some woman could love, but obviously he'd once been a different person. Grief had changed him.

"That's just terrible," Mary said in a near whisper. She wiped tears from her eyes.

"It really is awful," John said. "No wonder he acts the way he does. I know how hard it is to recover from that kind of heartbreak."

"He retired not long after that," Martha said. "Then he became the man we know now. I think he needs friends. He's shut himself off from everyone. It's made him mean and suspicious."

Elizabeth looked at her usually pragmatic sister. Uriah's story had touched her too.

"I agree," Mary said. "We can do something about that, can't we?"

Elizabeth shrugged. "Only if he'll let us."

"Ruth said they went by several times after Doris and Brandon died, but Uriah wouldn't talk to them. Down through the years, the church has continued to reach out to him, but he's repelled every attempt."

"Any idea why he disappeared for a year?" Elizabeth asked.

"No. Ruth didn't know anything about it." She sighed. "Getting him to open up to people again won't be easy."

"Well, he hasn't come up against the Classen sisters," Mary said with a wink. "He doesn't have a chance."

John grinned. "I have a feeling life is going to get very interesting for Uriah Barnhart."

They'd almost finished lunch when John's phone rang. The sisters listened as he answered it. John's responses to whatever he was hearing were noncommittal. After a few minutes, he thanked whoever had called him and hung up. "That was my friend, the one who knows about Civil War memorabilia," he said. "He's as sure as he can be that the sword never belonged to Stonewall Jackson. Jackson was famous for not using a sword, and there's no record of any other swords besides the one he wore regularly. As far as the value goes, it is from the Civil War, so he said he'd put a price of about two thousand dollars on it. Of course, that's retail. A seller would probably net around five hundred to one thousand."

Elizabeth tried to digest this information. If it was correct, and she had no reason to believe it wasn't, they were back at square one. At least it was worth a little more than George had suggested.

"So that's it," Martha said. "We have no idea what Warren's riddle means. It looks like we never will."

"That's no excuse for the way Anita's handled everything," Mary said, "but I really wanted to solve this." She looked at Elizabeth. "So now what? We give up?"

"I don't see what choice we have," she answered. "We've gone through every single item and haven't been able to figure it out yet."

"Have we really gone through everything?" Martha asked.

Elizabeth was surprised by her question. "I...I think so. Do you think we missed something?"

"As I see it, there are quite a few things we haven't considered. You know, like frying pans. Dish towels. Items that just *couldn't* be valuable. I say we go home and get out the list of everything Anita gave us. We'll compare each and every one with the riddle. After we've done that, we can truly say there's nothing left we can do. Then we can turn this back over to Anita with clear consciences."

Elizabeth carefully considered Martha's suggestion. Even though it was the last thing she wanted to do, it made sense. Finally, she said, "Okay. You're right. But after that we walk away, right? I don't want this hanging over our heads forever."

Martha and Mary nodded their agreement.

The group finished their lunch and headed home. Elizabeth should have felt relief since they were surely coming to the end of their search for Anita's missing treasure, but even though she wanted to be happy about it, she just couldn't. It was a mystery she'd wanted to solve. Now it looked as if it wouldn't happen—and that left her feeling unsatisfied.

CHAPTER THIRTY-TWO

That afternoon, the sisters gathered at the kitchen table with their inventory list. John had offered to help, so they went through every item one by one, even going to extreme measures in an attempt to match objects to the riddle. A few of them were humorous, like embroidered dish towels with robins. Mary's suggestion that it explained the feathers brought an outburst of laughter. At first, Mary insisted that a Smucker cousin could have made the towels, but then even she started to giggle at the absurdity of her suggestion.

It took almost three hours to go through the entire list. When Martha finally closed the book, she shook her head.

"That's it," she said. "Whatever Warren Smucker left behind isn't here. We need to tell Anita we simply can't find it. She needs to check all the things she still has. No matter what the appraiser she hired told her, either it's still in the house, it never existed, or Warren got rid of it before he died."

"There's just no indication he sold anything that valuable," Elizabeth said. She leaned back in her chair and reached for her coffee cup. "But I agree. We're done. There's just nothing else we can do."

"When do we tell Anita?" Mary asked.

"I'm going to call her now," Elizabeth said. "I should probably wait until tomorrow, but honestly, we need to start concentrating on the store. This whole thing has been a major distraction."

"And if she threatens us again?" Martha asked.

"I don't believe she will, but if she does, we'll just have to deal with it. We've done everything she's asked of us. Even when it was uncomfortable."

"You've gone above and beyond," John said. "Once she knows about the sword, at least she can stop obsessing about it."

"That's true," Elizabeth said. "But now she's without an answer. I'm praying she won't lose her house."

John smiled at her. "I probably ought to head for home. I don't want to overstay my welcome."

"You're not doing any such thing. Could you wait until after I call Anita? I want to get this done before I chicken out."

"Sure, I'll wait. Do you mind if I stretch my legs a bit? I'd like to look around outside."

"No, not at all. Just watch out for Reddy. He might resent your intrusion and chase after you."

John looked a little alarmed. "Who's Reddy? Is he the border collie? He seems friendly."

Mary giggled. "No, that's Pal. Reddy is our big red rooster. He thinks he owns this place."

John grinned. "I'll be careful. Thanks for the warning."

Martha stood up. "While you're meeting our critters, let me introduce you to our goats. You'll like them."

"I'm coming too," Mary said, getting up and going to the door. "Come on. We'll give you the tour."

John looked over at Elizabeth. "I guess I'll be outside meeting the goats."

She laughed. "I'll rescue you as soon as I can."

Mary and John went out the door with Martha following. Elizabeth went into the living room in case they came inside before she was finished. It would be much quieter. She took a deep breath and dialed Anita's number. The phone was picked up almost immediately.

"Hi, Anita," she said. "Are you busy?"

"No. What can I do for you?"

Anita's voice was muffled, and she sniffed several times. Maybe she had a cold. Elizabeth wondered if talking to her now was a good idea.

"Are you feeling okay?"

Another sniff. "I'm fine. I found the diary I told you about. I just finished reading it."

"You mean Gideon Smucker's diary?"

"Yes."

"You sound upset."

Anita's shuddering sigh came through the phone. "Oh, Elizabeth, Gideon wrote quite a bit about Noah Barnhart. How he saved his life more than once. They were so close. Like brothers. Everything Uriah has been saying all along is true. After Gideon's accounts stopped, Noah left one last entry. What happened really was a horrible accident. One that must have tortured Noah the rest of his life. It's very clear he never would have purposely hurt my great-great-grandfather. What happened broke his heart." She paused for a moment. "I'm afraid I owe Uriah an apology. Somehow, down through the years, my family seems to have twisted the story, making it sound as if Noah purposely killed Gideon. They obviously never read this diary. I think they assumed there wasn't anything but clothes in that trunk."

"I think Uriah would love to read the diary too, Anita."

"You're right. I'll contact him this week. See if he'll talk to me." She cleared her throat. "Has the sword been found?"

Elizabeth told her about the deliveryman from the dairy and that the sword was in the police's possession. "Once the investigation is over, the sword will be returned to Uriah," she said, wondering what Anita's reaction would be.

"That's fine. It's his. He paid for it. If it's the treasure my father left for me, it's my fault for letting it go after he told me not to sell it. Whatever happens, I'll deal with it."

Grateful for the opening, Elizabeth shared the information she'd gotten from John's friend.

"So it isn't the sword," Anita said softly.

"No, and we've gone through every single item you gave us, Anita. Whatever your father wanted you to have—it's just not here. All I can suggest is that you get another appraiser to go through what's left in the house. Maybe the first guy missed something, and someone else will figure it out."

"I don't know, Elizabeth," she said, her voice low. "I'm tired of looking. I can't solve the riddle, and I have no clue where this so-called treasure is—or if it even exists. Maybe it was just a figment of my father's imagination."

"I'm sorry. We really wanted to help you. I was so sure we'd figure this out."

"You did everything you could. Forgive me for being so terrible to you. None of this was your fault. It was all mine."

"It's fine. We're not upset with you. Just sad you didn't get a different outcome."

"Maybe you could all come here for dinner next week," Anita said. "I would feel better apologizing in person. And if you'll bring me a list of everyone who brought items back to you, I'll return them. I owe them all apologies too."

"I'd be happy to. I'm sure you'll find most of them aren't angry about it. People are pretty forgiving." As she said the words, she ran through the list of customers in her head. There were a couple of people she intended to talk to before Anita contacted them. They might need a little encouragement to be kind.

Elizabeth said goodbye and hung up. Then she sat for a while, just thinking. They could finally stop looking for Anita's elusive treasure. She was glad, but knowing Anita was still in financial trouble kept the victory from being one she could completely celebrate. And she still couldn't shake her disappointment at not being able to solve the mystery. She had to admit, she'd kind of enjoyed trying.

Finally, she put the phone down and went to the window to see John with the goats. Wynken and Nod were a little standoffish, but Blynken was obviously happy to have a new friend. He kept trying to jump up on poor John, who was simultaneously trying to pet the funny little goat and protect himself from injury.

Elizabeth grabbed a banana from the counter, went out on the porch, and put her fingers in her mouth. She let out a loud whistle. When Blynken heard it, he jumped down and ran behind his brother and sister.

"How did you do that?" John asked as she approached.

"Just training. Blynken knows that if he obeys my whistle, he'll get a treat." She started peeling the banana. The little goat ran over to her, looking up at Elizabeth with an expression so adoring, everyone laughed. She broke off a piece of the banana and fed it to the wide-eyed goat. Wynken and Nod ran over to get their fair share. Once they'd all gotten their treat, Elizabeth opened the gate and ushered everyone out of their pen.

"Where did you learn to whistle like that?" John asked. "Very impressive."

Elizabeth grinned. "Daddy taught his girls to whistle when we were kids. It comes in handy when you're working with farm animals."

"I guess so. You'll have to teach me that someday."

"You can't whistle?" Mary asked.

"I can whistle, but not like that. That's a super whistle. Maybe I could use it the next time I try to arrest someone who wants to argue with me. One loud whistle could shut them down."

Elizabeth chuckled. "I can teach you. Never thought I'd be an asset to law enforcement."

John's laugh made her smile. "What's over there?" he asked, pointing at an old storage shed.

"Daddy's old truck," Martha said. "We want to get it going again someday, but for now it just sits."

"Can I see it?"

Elizabeth nodded. "Sure." She turned to Mary. "Can you get the keys to the shed from the kitchen? They're in the junk drawer."

"You don't have to do that," John said. "I didn't realize you didn't have the keys."

"Nonsense," Mary said. "It won't take me but a minute to get them. I'll be right back."

Elizabeth led John toward the old weathered shed. Daddy had put it up years ago, but over time the paint had faded, and a few boards had split. The windows on either side were so dirty, it was impossible to see inside.

"This old shed needs work," she said. "Some repair and cleaning. It could also use a new coat of paint. We've been so busy working on the store there hasn't been time to tackle all the jobs around here that have to be done."

"I think these are the right ones," Mary said, trotting up next to Elizabeth. She held out a set of keys. "Is the shed key here?"

"Yeah, this is it." She slid the key into the lock and turned it. John helped pull the shed doors open. Light streamed in, but when the doors were pulled back, the movement stirred up layers of dust that filled the air, causing Elizabeth to cough. "It's been a while since we've been in here," she said.

"I guessed that," John said, clearing his throat. He walked over to the old green truck that was covered with dust. "Wow.

This is a classic. An old Ford truck. We've got to get this going again."

"We want to," Elizabeth said. "It means a lot to us. Daddy loved this truck."

"He was a Ford man," Martha said as she lovingly touched one of the fenders. "Was always telling us to buy Fords. 'You can always trust a Ford,' he used to tell us."

Elizabeth started to say something when she suddenly stopped and stared at her sisters.

"Lizzie?" Mary said. "Are you okay? You've gone completely white."

Elizabeth slowly nodded. "I'm not only all right, I believe I might very well know where Anita's treasure is."

CHAPTER THIRTY-THREE

Can I get you something to drink?" Anita asked, addressing the Classen sisters, who were gathered together in her living room Sunday evening.

"I'm fine," Elizabeth said.

Martha and Mary also turned down her offer. Elizabeth was certain it was because they felt the same way she did—too excited to think about anything else.

"I'm...I'm not sure why you're here," Anita said, her forehead slightly furrowed. "We just talked on the phone a little while ago. I told you, Elizabeth, that I understood why you had to quit trying to solve my father's riddle."

"That's just it," Elizabeth said. She took a deep breath, trying to calm her jangled nerves. "We found it, Anita."

Anita's eyes widened, and her mouth dropped open. "What? What did you say?"

"I said that we found it. We found your treasure."

"I...what? You...you found it?" Immediately her eyes filled with tears. "Are you sure? Please don't tell me this if you're not sure."

"I'm absolutely certain." Elizabeth leaned forward in her chair. "We looked for hidden value in everything you gave us. In the end, it was the thing that seemed to have the least value that turned out to be incredibly significant."

"I don't understand."

Elizabeth cleared her throat. "First of all, let's look at your father's riddle." She opened her purse and pulled out the folded sheet of paper they'd studied time and time again. "No matter how hard we tried to make this fit all kinds of different things, it just didn't. In the end, we were willing to assume your father was a little...confused when he wrote it. So we tried to make it fit loosely to...something. That became the sword. It was the only thing that made a little sense, but after a while, we discovered the sword couldn't be the answer. That's when we gave up. But then something happened—"

"Our daddy's truck," Mary said with a wide smile.

"Truck?" Anita looked confused. "What are you talking about?"

Elizabeth shot Mary a look, but she couldn't be upset with her for jumping ahead. They were all too wound up. Elizabeth's heart was beating so hard, it was amazing it didn't leap out of her chest. She stared down at the sheet of paper and began to read. *"When lightning speaks and feathers fly, And your mother's sister's child makes dirty pies, You'll find yourself feeling quite continental. Open your eyes, and you'll see the truth. Hidden in shadows and very sentimental.'"* She looked up at Anita. "I'm going to explain each and every line. You tell me when you understand what the riddle means."

Anita frowned at her. "All right. If I can."

"Actually, we were close to solving it a couple of times. Mary and Martha both had it right, but like you, we decided the riddle couldn't have anything to do with vehicles. You weren't selling any cars or trucks. But that's exactly what your father was trying to get you to see." She nervously cleared her throat. "We solved the first two lines correctly. Well, kind of correctly. 'When lightning speaks and feathers fly'...it's a thunderbird. But not some kind of mythical bird. It's the car. A Thunderbird made by..."

"Ford!" Mary said.

"Mary, hush," Martha hissed. "Let Elizabeth explain this in her own way."

Mary leaned back in her chair and sighed deeply. "She's taking too long," she mumbled.

Elizabeth couldn't help but laugh at her fidgety sister. "Yes, that's right. Ford. And of course your mother's sister's child is your..."

"Cousin," Anita said.

"Right. And what is a dirty pie made of? We made them when we were kids."

Anita blinked a few times as if she was thinking. "Mud pies?"

"Exactly. Then we get to 'you'll find yourself feeling quite continental.'"

Anita shrugged. "I'm not sure..."

"Again, think of it in terms of a car."

"A Lincoln Continental?" she asked.

"Yes. Then your father talks about something hidden in shadows. And something very sentimental. And he was right. The answer has to do with something that means a lot to us. To all of us."

Anita threw her hands up in the air. "I still don't get it."

"Let's look at the words, okay? What are they?"

Anita rubbed her forehead for a moment. "Ford...cousin...mud...Lincoln...and something sentimental."

Elizabeth didn't say anything for a moment, she just waited.

A strange look passed across Anita's face, and she leaned forward in her chair. "Ford? Ford's Theater? The theater where Lincoln was assassinated? The play that night was *Our American Cousin.*" She frowned for a moment. "Mud? Samuel Mudd? The doctor who conspired with John Wilkes Booth? And of course, Lincoln's shooting was sentimental. He was a very beloved president." She clasped her hands together. "But how do shadows have anything to do with this?"

Elizabeth bent down and removed a large envelope from her purse. She carefully extracted a photo from it. "When you gave us that gaudy picture frame to sell, we never really looked at the picture in it. A quick glance at a couple we didn't know. The woman who bought the frame tossed the picture on the floor. Thankfully, we found it before it was damaged." She carefully handed the photo to Anita, who shrugged when she looked at it.

"This couple is related to us somehow, but I have no idea who they are. That's why I didn't keep the picture, although I probably should have kept the frame. I bought it for my father when I was five. It was the very first gift I ever gave him. Of course, it was cheap and gaudy. He only used it because he didn't want to hurt my feelings."

"Look at the photo again," Elizabeth said. "In front of the theater—and then in the shadows."

As Anita refocused on the photo, she gasped. "Oh my goodness," she said breathlessly.

"That's President Lincoln and his wife in front of the theater. They must have just gotten out of their carriage."

"And in the shadows..."

Anita stared closer at the photo. Then she suddenly looked up at Elizabeth, amazement on her face. "It's him, isn't it? Standing in the portico? Isn't that John Wilkes Booth?"

Elizabeth shrugged. "I'm not sure, Anita. But if it is, you might have the only photo of Booth and Lincoln together shortly before the shooting. I can't even imagine how valuable it is. It's... Well... it's probably priceless."

Tears slipped down Anita's face as she gazed at the photo. "And someone actually threw this on the floor?"

"It almost went in the trash," Mary said. "Elizabeth was smart enough to hang on to it just in case you decided you might want it back."

"Oh, Elizabeth. Thank you," Anita said, her voice breaking. "I wish my father would have just told me about this photo. His love of riddles almost cost me this priceless photo."

"It almost cost America this picture," Martha said. "I'm sure it will end up in a museum for all of us to see."

"I'll contact the appraiser I've been working with. He can help me get it to auction." She smiled. "But I'll make sure it ends up somewhere where everyone can experience it." Through her tears, she slid the photo back into the envelope. "I can't believe my father put something this priceless into that ugly old frame."

"Don't you understand, Anita?" Elizabeth said. "That frame was important to him because you gave it to him. With all his valuable antiques, that old frame was *his* greatest treasure. That's why he put your treasure inside of it."

Anita lowered her head and sobbed. "That means more to me than anything he could possibly have left for me," she choked out. Then she looked up at Elizabeth. "I think I'll keep that frame. Suddenly it seems incredibly beautiful."

"It really is."

"I have to ask how you finally figured this out. You told me you'd given up."

Elizabeth laughed. "Actually our father solved it. Or rather, his love of Ford cars and trucks." She told Anita about showing John the truck. "As we began to tell him how dedicated Daddy was to Ford, I thought back to all the different kinds of Ford vehicles we'd had. I remembered that the one car he always wanted, he never got. A Ford Thunderbird. Suddenly, the riddle began to come together. The word *continental* became a car too. The Lincoln Continental. The rest of it was easy once I had the word *Lincoln*."

"But at that point you didn't have anything that related to Lincoln."

"That's right, but your father said something about opening our eyes and seeing the truth. Suddenly, I remembered the picture. I'd noticed a theater behind the people in the photo, but I hadn't looked at it closely. Could it be Ford's Theater? I have to say I wasn't sure I was right but I went to find the picture just in case." She laughed nervously. "To be honest, for a while I couldn't remember where I put it. But I finally found it in a drawer in the desk in my room.

Once I looked past the couple, I could *see the truth*, as your father said."

"I'm not sure that picture would have occurred to me," Martha said. "I mean, even if I'd noticed the theater."

"Actually, something Mary said when we first saw the picture clicked in my memory. Do you recall what you said, Mary?"

She shook her head slowly. "Honestly, I barely remember looking at it."

"You said it wasn't a great shot. When I looked at it, I saw what you meant. The woman in the photo had her eyes closed. I'd noticed it the first time I saw the picture, but it didn't sink in until I realized it fit the riddle."

Mary snapped her fingers. "Oh yeah. I remember now. I assumed it was one of the reasons Anita didn't care about the picture."

"I really don't know how to thank you," Anita said. "I want to give you part of the money from the sale of the photo. A finder's fee. You deserve it."

"We appreciate that," Elizabeth said. "But there is one other thing you could do that would mean a great deal to us."

"Anything. What is it?"

"You can do what you said. You know, about making up with Uriah. And after you do, we'd like both of you to come over to our house for dinner."

"I'll go over there tomorrow. Hopefully, he'll see me."

"If you start out with what you learned from the diary, I'm sure he'll be happy to talk to you. And tell him the sword is his. That you have no interest in getting it back."

"I'll do that happily."

The sisters said goodbye and left. Although they were quiet on the way home, Elizabeth knew they were all satisfied with the outcome of their adventure. Maybe now things would settle down. She was certainly ready for life to become a little less exciting.

CHAPTER THIRTY-FOUR

Monday morning when the store opened, Elizabeth felt as if they'd been handed a brand-new beginning. At the same time, without Anita Smucker's treasure hunt hanging over their heads, around noon, life began to feel a little boring. She'd spent so much time trying to solve Warren's riddle, it was hard to redirect her mind to something else.

"Quit it, Elizabeth," she murmured to herself as she marked some new items going on the shelves.

Mary walked up to her. "Go on and have lunch," she said. "I've got this. Martha can come out when she's ready."

Elizabeth thanked her and started toward the door when a familiar car pulled up. Anita. For just a moment, Elizabeth tensed. She had to remind herself that there wasn't anything left for Anita to be angry about. Maybe she wanted to share news about the sale of the photo. However, instead of looking triumphant, her expression made it clear she was upset. What now?

"Can I speak to you for a minute?" she asked Elizabeth, "Outside?"

Elizabeth nodded and followed her to the door. Before she stepped out she glanced back at Mary, who stared at her in confusion. Elizabeth smiled, hoping to reassure her younger sister. After all, how could anything be wrong? The mystery had been solved.

Anita took Elizabeth's arm and pulled her a few yards away from the shop's entrance. Some people coming in looked their way, but they were too far away to hear their conversation.

"What's wrong?" Elizabeth asked, her voice wavering a little.

"Nothing with the photo," Anita said quickly. "Please don't look so worried. It's... It's Uriah. I went by his house this morning, and he wouldn't see me. I really want to find a way to bridge this gap, Elizabeth. I wondered... Would you go with me this afternoon? Please?"

Elizabeth felt a rush of relief—followed by a knot of concern in her stomach. "I don't know why you think he'll talk to me. The last time I saw him he was accusing me of stealing his sword."

"But you also helped recover it, right?"

"Well, yes. I guess I did."

"So maybe he'll be grateful." Anita sighed. "Look, I don't want to put you on the spot, but I really want to apologize to him. I need your help to do that."

Elizabeth had told John she and her sisters would wear Uriah down until he finally allowed them into his life. This wasn't the way she'd planned to do it, but maybe it was God's way. "Okay," she said slowly. "I'll go. But don't expect too much. It might take a while to get him to open up to us."

"I know he's angry with me, but I've heard he pushes everyone away. What made him so unsociable? Do you have any idea?"

Since Ruth hadn't asked them to keep what she'd shared quiet, Elizabeth told Anita about Uriah's sad past. By the time she finished, tears flowed down Anita's cheeks. Elizabeth couldn't hide her own emotions and dabbed at her eyes with her fingertips.

"Oh, Elizabeth. Now I feel even worse about the way our families have treated each other."

"There's no way you could have known about Uriah's fiancée and her grandson. And you didn't start the war between your families. Please don't beat yourself up. Uriah is responsible for his own actions, Anita. A lot of people have tragedy in their lives, but they don't isolate themselves and treat people with disrespect."

"I know. But I don't think what happened between our great-great-grandfathers helped anything."

"Well, let's see what we can do about that." She smiled at Anita. "Why don't we pray before we leave? I think we need all the help we can get."

"I think that's a wonderful idea."

The two women held hands and asked God to help them get through to Uriah Barnhart—to soften his heart and allow them to touch his life with God's love. When they said amen, Elizabeth felt better. Nothing was impossible with God. With His love, maybe they could help to heal Uriah's broken heart.

They got into Anita's car then drove over to Uriah's, parking in front of his house.

"Since he told me to leave," Anita said, "could you talk to him alone first? Maybe he'll listen to you."

Although she didn't want to face Uriah by herself, Elizabeth agreed. "If I can get us both inside, I'll wave at you," she said.

"Okay." Anita put her hand on Elizabeth's arm. "Bless you for trying, Elizabeth. I believe God is with you."

Elizabeth got out of the car. She stood looking at the old house for a moment, praying Anita was right. She took a deep breath and started walking up the sidewalk. She'd just stepped up on the porch when the front door swung open. Uriah stood there, glaring at her. His expression was menacing, not the reaction she'd hoped for.

"The police haven't returned the sword yet," he barked. "So you're wasting your time. I'm not letting it out of my sight again. Ever."

"That's fine, Mr. Barnhart," she said. "I'm not here about the sword."

"Then why are you here?" he asked in a loud voice. "Do I have something else you want?"

"No." Elizabeth blew out the breath she'd been holding. "Look, I want to... I mean we want to—"

"We? Who's we?" He stepped out on the porch and stared at the car. "Is that Anita Smucker? You brought her with you?"

"She asked me to come here with her. She needs to talk to you, Mr. Barnhart. She wants—"

"She wants my sword!" He shook his fist at the car. "She's not getting it. I told you—"

"Uriah, stop it. Stop it right now." Elizabeth almost gasped at her own words. Where had that come from? And she'd called him by his first name. Now she'd done it.

"What…what do you want?" he asked, his face white as a sheet.

Although she didn't understand the change in his demeanor, she decided to push forward. "I want to come in and talk to you. Like two civilized adults. I *don't* want to stand out here yelling."

He stepped back toward the door. Elizabeth was shocked to see him pull the door open and gesture for her to come inside. When she did, he walked into the living room and sat down on the couch without saying a word. She lowered herself into a chair near him.

"I need you to listen to me for a couple of minutes," Elizabeth said. "That's it. If you want me to leave and never come back, I'll respect your wishes."

He didn't respond, but he waved his hand as if telling her to continue.

"Anita Smucker has come here today to talk to you, not to ask for the sword. She doesn't want it. She only wants to apologize to you."

His bushy eyebrows shot up. "Apologize to me? For what?"

"For the animosity that's existed between your families. She has something to show you. A diary written by Gideon Smucker. In it, he talks about the great friendship he had with Noah, your great-great-grandfather. He said Noah had saved his life more than once. He loved Noah like a brother. After Gideon died, Noah was almost inconsolable. We know this because of the last entry in the diary, written by Noah himself. In the end, he could only go on because he believed it's what Gideon would have wanted. I don't know if you're aware of this, but he named one of his children Gideon, in honor of his dear friend. The anger that the Smuckers have had toward Noah was misplaced, Uriah. You were right, and Anita is really sorry for it. She wants to see if you two can heal the rift in your families. I think it's time, isn't it?"

He was quiet for a moment. "I'll talk to her. You can tell her to come inside."

Although she was thrilled to hear it, Elizabeth was confused by the sudden change in his attitude. "I have to ask you something. When I told you on the porch to stop arguing with me, you seemed...surprised. Why?" Truthfully, Elizabeth was just as stunned as Uriah. She never talked that way to anyone. Especially someone she was a little afraid of.

Suddenly the old man's eyes filled with tears. "There was a woman once who would set me straight when I needed it. At that moment you sounded just like her." He shook his head. "I realized that if she were here, that's exactly what she would have said to me." He met Elizabeth's gaze. "I don't want to be angry anymore. It's exhausting. I've been angry ever since I lost someone...two people...years ago. I'm not honoring their memories. I'm making it worse." His shaky sigh was full of emotion. "A year ago I found out I had cancer. I went to Philadelphia for treatment. I've never felt so alone in my life. The cancer's gone, but my doctor told me if I didn't get rid of my rage, it could come back. He believes that sometimes our state of mind can affect our bodies. I think he's right. I can't say I've felt good for years." He stood up. "Look, I want you to know that it wasn't just the way you talked to me on the porch. Your mother was the only other person I ever trusted. She had a way of seeing beyond my facade. I liked her, and she really liked me, although there wasn't any reason to."

"The Zooks like you too," Elizabeth said. "They won't be at the church much longer. They'll be leaving soon. I know they'd love to see you before they go."

"One step at a time," Uriah said, "but I'll try." Then he did something Elizabeth had never seen from him. Uriah Barnhart smiled.

Blinking away fresh tears, Elizabeth picked up her purse and headed for the front door. "I'll send Anita in." She paused with her hand on the door. "I have your phone number, you know. I hope that's okay. I'll be calling you soon. My sisters and I want you to come to our house for supper." She turned around and grinned at him. "And I expect you to come, Uriah."

He nodded and wiped the tears from his eyes. "I'll be there. Thank you."

As Elizabeth walked toward the car where Anita waited, she quietly thanked God for her life in Bird-in-Hand, her sisters, and all the unexpected blessings that had come out of what had at first looked like a trial. Slowly but surely, she was discovering who she was again. She'd found out she wasn't too old for new beginnings, that the Classen sisters were a formidable team, and that Jessica Fletcher had nothing on her.

She had hope that good days were ahead, and she could hardly wait to see all the surprises God had in store for them.

A NOTE FROM THE AUTHOR

I love the setting of Bird-in-Hand, Pennsylvania, for my novel, *Another's Treasure*, book one in the Mysteries of Lancaster County series. Readers will enjoy finding out more about Bird-in-Hand and the people who call the quaint village home. Bird-in-Hand is a tiny place with a big heart. Lots of great restaurants, bakeries, gift shops, and special events for tourists. We hope to introduce you to many of them as we follow the Classen sisters' stories.

I also believe readers will love Elizabeth, Martha, and Mary, who run Secondhand Blessings, a thrift store that has been in their family for generations. We have a great lineup of talented authors who will propel the sisters into intricate mysteries while introducing you to unique and colorful characters.

As with every Guideposts cozy mystery series, I'm privileged to work with several incredible authors, but I'm also very excited to announce that I'll be teaming up with my talented daughter-in-law, Shaen Layle. You'll enjoy her wonderful writing. What a joy for me to write with a woman who is not only my daughter-in-law but also my dear friend.

I know you'll love this series. I'm so honored to be a part of it!

Nancy Mehl

ABOUT THE AUTHOR

Nancy Mehl is a best-selling, award-winning author who lives in Missouri with her husband, Norman, and her puggle, Watson. She's authored over thirty books and is currently writing a new series for Bethany House Publishing. The Kaely Quinn Profiler series released book one, *Mind Games,* in December 2018. She has also written for a cozy mystery series for Guideposts, the Mysteries of Martha's Vineyard.

Readers can learn more about Nancy through her website: www.nancymehl.com. She is part of The Suspense Sisters: www.suspensesisters.blogspot.com, along with several other popular suspense authors. She is also very active on Facebook.

BARN FINDS

My husband and I love yard sales and secondhand stores. We've found so many great treasures. I always look for Pyrex baking dishes, and Norman, who is a musician, searches for items to add to his music studio.

We've found a lot of great deals. Once Norman bought a very valuable speaker for $25.00 from a guy who was once on a popular TV talent show.

But the greatest thing I found at a secondhand store was a Raggedy Ann that looked just like the one I'd had when I was a little girl! I loved that doll until she fell apart. Down through the years I wished several times that I'd kept her, maybe even tried to have her restored. Then a few months ago, Norman and I were looking through a rather large secondhand store. I was walking down the aisles and rounded a corner. There she was, just sitting on the shelf as if waiting for me. Of course, I bought her, and now she sits on the rocking chair in my office, smiling at me as if saying, "I missed you too, but now we're together again."

That might sound silly to you, but if you've ever had a favorite doll you had to say goodbye to...I think you'll understand.

FRESH FROM MARTHA'S KITCHEN

Martha's Pumpkin Bread

Ingredients

1⅔ cups all-purpose flour

1½ cups sugar

1 teaspoon baking soda

1 teaspoon ground cinnamon

¾ teaspoon salt

½ teaspoon baking powder

½ teaspoon ground nutmeg

¼ teaspoon ground cloves

2 large eggs, room temperature

1 cup canned pumpkin

½ cup canola oil

½ cup water

½ cup chopped walnuts, optional

½ cup raisins, optional

Directions

Preheat oven to 350°. Combine first eight ingredients. Whisk together eggs, pumpkin, oil, and water; stir into dry ingredients just until moistened. Fold in walnuts and raisins, if desired.

Pour into a greased 9 × 5-inch loaf pan. Bake until a toothpick inserted in center comes out clean, 65 to 70 minutes. Cool in pan 10 minutes before removing to a wire rack.

Read on for an exciting sneak peek of another
Mysteries of Lancaster County book

Garage Sale Secret
by Elizabeth Ludwig

Mary Classen Baxter lifted her face to the sky and let the rising sun's rays warm her skin. Still hard to believe, but here she was, on the farm where she grew up. After so many years away, she was finally adjusting to living back in Bird-in-Hand. She'd been back three months now, and truth be told, it wasn't so bad. Mary sighed in contentment and flicked away a persistent fly that appeared determined to land on her nose. She relished the slower pace than her old life in Indianapolis, the fresh air, and the camaraderie flourishing between herself and her sisters. She was even getting used to Reddy's gentle nudge prying her from sleep.

As if on cue, the family rooster crowed, breaking the early morning silence.

"You're too late, Reddy," she called, cupping her hand to her mouth. "I'm awake."

Reddy's raucous song flowed on, uninterrupted. Mary smiled. The old bird would soon have everyone in the house up and moving. Her dachshund, Tinkerbelle, or Tink, as she affectionately called her, didn't much care for Reddy. She lifted her head and sent a low growl in the direction of the barn.

"Crazy rooster. Good thing I've already put the coffee on, huh?" she said, reaching down to rub Tink behind the ears.

Tink gazed up at her, her tail thumping the porch. Stretching one last time, Mary turned and pulled open the screen door, its grumpy screech adding harmony to Reddy's chorus. From the rear of the house, pots and pans clattered. Apparently, Martha was up before the old rooster's alarm too.

Mary laid the morning newspaper on the hall table and stopped to take a deep breath in through her nose. Was that bacon she smelled? She changed into her house slippers and headed for the kitchen with her mouth watering.

Martha eyed her over the pancake batter she was whisking. "You're up early."

Mary pulled a coffee cup from the cupboard. "I have an errand I need to run before church, so I gave myself a little extra time to get the animals fed and watered."

The pancake batter hissed as it hit the griddle. Somehow, Martha always managed to get her pancakes perfectly round, a trick Mary had never mastered. Not that she had need of the skill now, with Martha's excellent cooking keeping them all fed.

"Are you going to the cemetery after the service?" Martha set the batter bowl aside and reached for a spatula. She jabbed it toward a platter of bacon. "Get yourself a slice."

Mary happily obliged. She bit off a piece and chewed it. "Yeah, I thought I would stop by. Hey, do you suppose that old caretaker—what was his name—still works there?"

"Duffy Porter?" Martha waited a moment and then deftly flipped the pancake. "No idea. Why?"

"I was thinking about planting a dogwood and maybe setting a little bench next to it, but I don't know what the rules are regarding that type of thing. I thought I would check with him first."

Martha put a finished pancake on the platter with the others. "You've always loved visiting that cemetery, even before we laid Daddy and now Mama to rest there."

Mary finished off the bacon, and then wiped her hands on a paper towel. "It's so peaceful and calm there. The wind rustles through the trees... the setting is beautiful and perfect for painting... I like it."

Spying Martha's grimace, Mary chuckled. She and her sisters were alike in many ways, but this was definitely not one of them. She grabbed three plates from the cupboard and set them next to the griddle, then went to the refrigerator for the butter. She set it and a knife next to the plates before turning toward the pantry.

"Hey, do we have any more of that all-natural maple syrup Lizzie bought from the craft fair?"

"Second shelf," Martha called.

Mary found it and carried it back to the counter where Martha had two steaming pancakes waiting on a plate.

She pushed the plate toward Mary and slid two more pancakes onto the second plate for herself. "So what time do you think you'll be back from the cemetery? I heard there was a large estate sale over near New Holland. I was thinking about going."

Estate sales were fun, but Mary shook her head and pointed to the satchel hanging on a hook next to the door.

"Probably better go without me. I was thinking of taking my paintbrushes."

Martha sighed, and Mary knew why. Used to be Mary would lose all track of time when she was sitting in front of an easel. Granted, it had been a long time since she'd devoted herself to her art, but she was hoping it would be that way again once she got a little paint on her fingers.

She gobbled her breakfast, poured a second cup of coffee into an insulated travel mug, picked up her satchel, and headed toward the door.

"Mary?"

Mary hiked the satchel strap higher and looked over her shoulder at Martha. Martha pointed at Mary's feet. "Your shoes."

"What? Oh." Mary looked down with a giggle and wiggled her toes. She was still wearing her slippers. "Guess I should change, huh?"

Her sister's laughter echoing in her ears, Mary dashed up the stairs to her closet, shoved her feet into a sturdy pair of boots, and then continued on her way. She made a quick stop for gas and a birthday card for her Sunday school teacher before heading to church. Thankfully, the early service was a lot more relaxed than the more traditional one that took place after. Her boots and casual slacks were not out of place there.

After the service concluded, she slipped away from the people lingering and chatting in the foyer and headed for the cemetery. A light breeze rustled through the leaves on the trees as she exited her car and wound down the narrow path toward her parents' graves. Instantly, a sense of peace lifted her spirits. Granted, it *was* mingled with a tiny bit of sorrow and a smidgeon of loneliness for her father's full laugh and her mother's gentle wisdom, but it was peace nonetheless.

She slowed as she passed a row of grave markers bearing familiar names. There was a stone for her old high school English teacher, and one for a former pastor of their church. Farther down were two identical stones for the twin boys who had died one summer in a boating accident when Mary was a teenager. There was even an elegant marble stone for Wavel Hebert, the curmudgeonly owner of the diner where Mary used to drink root beer floats and chat with her friends—that was, when old Wavel wasn't chasing them out. She smiled. That was the thing about small towns. Everyone knew everyone.

Finally, she reached her parents' graves, and her eyes filled with tears at the words etched into the headstone.

Beloved Father and Mother.

Yes, they were beloved as parents, but they were so much more. Mentors. Friends. Cheerleaders. Even during the rough spots.

"It doesn't matter how old you are, when your parents pass away, you still feel like an orphan."

Her mother's words struck a poignant chord in Mary's heart. Her mother had whispered them at Grandma Lois's funeral nearly a decade ago, but Mary remembered it as though she'd spoken them yesterday.

"You were right, Mama," she whispered, running her hand over the name etched into the marble. "I do feel like an orphan sometimes."

Nearby, a bird's chirrup drew her from her melancholy. He lit on a large black headstone, eyed her for a moment with his little blue head cocked to one side, and then set about preening. Apparently he didn't view her as a threat.

Mary smiled, slid her phone carefully from her pocket, and snapped a quick picture to study later. Disturbed by the sound, her feathered friend tweeted his displeasure before fluttering off in a flurry of wings. Ah, well. At least she'd have the picture.

She enlarged the photo, glad to see she'd captured a crisp likeness. Oftentimes, her attempts at phone photography came out blurry. Still, carrying a phone was a lot easier than lugging a three-pound Polaroid around her neck.

Enlarging the photo had the added benefit of enlarging the name carved into the headstone. Mary frowned. Paul Classen. Uncle Paul. She looked up at the marker and then back down at her phone. She'd forgotten he was buried up there. Suddenly, it struck her as really sad and lonely.

Leaving the cluster of family markers, Mary struck up the sloping hill toward his grave. When she reached it, she paused to catch her breath, her hands braced firmly on her hips.

She looked back downhill. "That was quite a hike."

And why? It really was odd that he was buried so far from the rest of the family. If she'd been told the reason why, it escaped her now.

"At least the view from up here is beautiful, eh, Uncle Paul?"

She rested her hand atop his tombstone. Below them, acres of rich farmland stretched to the farthest corners of Lancaster County. In the distance, pale white silos poked at the sky.

She sighed happily and pulled her satchel off her shoulder. This would be a perfect spot to get her creative juices flowing. She lowered herself to the ground, took out her brushes and a few tubes of paint, and got to work. Before long, she'd lost herself in the almost hypnotic strokes of her brush across the canvas.

"Pretty."

Mary jumped and let out a small shriek. The movement sent her hand skittering upward, creating an ugly dark slash across her otherwise lovely painting. She stared at it in dismay.

"Ooh...sorry about that. I didn't mean to startle you." The owner of the voice smiled, exposing deep dimples on either side of his mouth.

"Th-that's all right," Mary stammered as she collected her paints and threw them into her satchel. "I was concentrating and didn't hear you walk up."

The man watched her with a remorseful frown. "I hope you're not leaving because of me." He hefted a rake in one hand. "I've got to get back to work. I just noticed you up here painting and...well..."

He shrugged shyly and waved his hand at the area surrounding them. Mary followed his gaze. Obviously, he'd been working in a wide circle around her for some time. Piles of branches, grass clippings, and debris lay scattered about. No doubt he'd been wondering when, if ever, she'd be finished.

"I'm so sorry." Mary threw the rest of her belongings into her bag and tossed the strap over her shoulder. "I was completely absorbed in my painting. I get like that when I'm working."

"Me too." He chuckled and stuck out his hand. "Name's Rafe Porter."

Mary gave his hand a shake. He had a strong grip, but his palms weren't nearly as calloused as she might have expected from a gardener. And why was he working on a Sunday, anyway? Too shy to ask, she pulled her hand away and crossed her arms. "Mary Baxter."

He leaned his arms atop his rake. "I don't think I've met you before. Are you from around here, Mary Baxter?"

She nodded. "I grew up here. My name used to be Classen."

He straightened, and his gaze fell to Uncle Paul's headstone. "Classen, as in..."

"He was my uncle."

"Really?" His eyes gleamed with genuine interest. "So then, maybe *you* could tell me why Paul Classen is buried way up here when all the other Classens are down there." He inclined his head down the hill. "I've always wondered about it."

She shrugged and grinned wryly. "You'll have to keep wondering, I'm afraid. It's a mystery, even to me. My uncle died before I was born."

His wiggled his eyebrows. "I love a good mystery."

What could she say to that? Mary nodded lamely. "Me too." She gripped the strap on her satchel tightly. "So, Porter, huh? Any relation to Duffy Porter?"

"He's my uncle." Rafe gestured around the cemetery. "I know it's Sunday, but I had the afternoon free, so I figured I'd come by. I try and give Uncle Duffy a hand now and then, whenever he complains that his sciatica is giving him trouble."

So he didn't actually work here. That explained his nice hands. Just *hands*, she corrected quickly. Whether they were nice or not was irrelevant.

Their eyes met, and worried he might see her thoughts reflected there, Mary pointed toward the far corner of the cemetery where the caretaker's cottage was located. "Well, it's been some time since I've seen your uncle, but from what I remember, you certainly look like him. I remember him smiling a lot and..." She motioned rather bashfully toward Rafe's thick salt-and-pepper locks. "He had good hair."

Good hair? Good grief! She stifled a groan.

He laughed then—a rich, deep sound that invited her to smile with him.

He bent and retrieved her painting, lingering over it a moment before he gave it to her. "So you're a painter, huh?"

Her face warmed. She took the painting gingerly so as not to smudge the paint not already marred by the slash of brown. "It's a hobby. I'm just now getting back into it."

"Really? You're good. I would have thought you did it professionally."

More heat crept up her neck. "Thank you."

He pointed to the canvas. "I'm really sorry about messing you up. Can you fix it?"

"I can try. I'll have to look at it again when I get home."

He nodded. "I hope so. It's really beautiful. And the mark almost looks like a person standing there looking out over the view."

Mary's gaze dropped to the painting. Indeed, she could almost imagine it as he described. And from here, the vantage would be her uncle's. Melancholy took hold of her as she imagined him standing in this very spot, looking down over the family plots—alone. Isolated. Lonely. Why hadn't she ever bothered to find out what happened?

"Oops. I've lost you."

She blinked and drew her gaze back to Rafe. "Sorry."

He lifted one hand. "Nope, I interrupted you. No need to apologize. I should be getting back to work anyway."

He lingered despite his words, a look of curiosity on his handsome face.

Again, with the adjectives!

Mary squeezed the strap on her satchel as her thoughts winged to Bill Richmond, an old friend she'd reconnected with here. "Well, it was nice meeting you, Rafe. Please tell your uncle hello for me."

"Will do." He shifted the rake to his other hand, and a smile stretched his lips. "It was nice meeting you too, Mary."

Mary turned and hurried down the hill. *Crumbs.* What was it about Rafe Porter that set her on edge? She hadn't felt this way since—

She shuddered as she reached her car and tossed her satchel inside. Of course she remembered the last time she'd felt this way. It had turned out to be a complete disaster, and she had vowed never, ever to let herself feel that way again.

A NOTE FROM THE EDITORS

We hope you enjoy Mysteries of Lancaster County, created by the Books and Inspirational Media Division of Guideposts, a nonprofit organization that touches millions of lives every day through products and services that inspire, encourage, help you grow in your faith, and celebrate God's love in every aspect of your daily life.

Thank you for making a difference with your purchase of this book, which helps fund our many outreach programs to military personnel, prisons, hospitals, nursing homes, and educational institutions. To learn more, visit GuidepostsFoundation.org.

We also maintain many useful and uplifting online resources. Visit Guideposts.org to read true stories of hope and inspiration, access OurPrayer network, sign up for free newsletters, download free e-books, join our Facebook community, and follow our stimulating blogs.

To learn about other Guideposts publications, including the best-selling devotional *Daily Guideposts*, go to ShopGuideposts.org, call (800) 932-2145, or write to Guideposts, PO Box 5815, Harlan, Iowa 51593.